THE SECRET THAT CAN'T BE HIDDEN

CAITLIN CREWS

MILLS & BOON

First published in Great Britain 2021
by Mills & Boon, an imprint of HarperCollins*Publishers* Ltd,
1 London Bridge Street, London, SE1 9GF

www.harpercollins.co.uk

HarperCollins*Publishers*
1st Floor, Watermarque Building,
Ringsend Road, Dublin 4, Ireland

Large Print edition 2021

The Secret That Can't Be Hidden © 2021 Caitlin Crews

ISBN: 978-0-263-28876-6

07/21

MIX
Paper from
responsible sources
FSC™ C007454

This book is produced from independently certified
FSC™ paper to ensure responsible forest management.
For more information visit www.harpercollins.co.uk/green.

Printed and bound in Great Britain
by CPI Group (UK) Ltd, Croydon, CR0 4YY

THE SECRET THAT
CAN'T BE HIDDEN

CHAPTER ONE

IF SHE CONCENTRATED on how outrageous the situation was, how humiliating and impossible, Kendra Connolly knew she would never do what needed to be done.

Yet there was no way around it. She had to do this.

Her family was depending on her—for the first time. Ever.

She'd been sitting in her car for far too long already in the parking structure deep beneath Skalas Tower in the hectic bustle of Midtown Manhattan. She'd been given a certain amount of time to appear on the cameras in the elevators before the security officials who'd checked her in would investigate her whereabouts, here beneath the North American power center of one of the world's wealthiest men. The clock was ticking, yet here she was, gripping the steering wheel while staring at her knuckles as they turned white. Psyching herself up for the unpleasant task ahead.

And failing.

"There must be some other solution," she had said to her father.

So many times, in fact, that it had really been a lot more like begging.

Kendra was desperate to avoid...this. But Thomas Pierpont Connolly had been unmoved, as ever.

"For God's sakes, Kendra," he had boomed at her earlier today, when she'd tried one last time to change his mind. He'd been leaning back in his monstrously oversized leather chair, his hands laced over his straining golf shirt because nothing kept him from a few holes at Wee Burn when he was in the family home on the Connecticut island his Gilded Age forebears had claimed long ago. "Think about someone other than yourself, for a change. Your brother needs your help. That should be the beginning and the end of it, girl."

Kendra hadn't dared say that she disagreed with that assessment of the situation. Not directly.

Tommy Junior had always been a problem, but their father refused to see it. To him, Tommy had always been made of spun gold. When he'd been expelled from every boarding school on the East Coast, Thomas had called him *high-spirited*. When he'd been kicked out of college—despite the library Thomas had built to get him in—it had been excused as *that Connolly bullheadedness*. His failed gestures toward entrepreneurial independence that cost his father several fortunes were seen as admirable attempts to follow in the family footsteps. His lackadaisical carrying-on as vice president of the family business—all expense account and very little actual work—was lauded by Thomas as *playing the game*.

Tommy Junior could literally do no wrong, though he'd certainly tried his best.

Kendra, meanwhile, had been an afterthought in her parents' polite, yet frosty marriage. Born when Tommy was fourteen and already on his fifth boarding school, her well-to-do parents had never known what to do with her. She'd been shunted off to nannies, which had suited her fine. The old Connolly fortune that consumed her father's and brother's lives had been meaningful to her only in that it provided the sprawling house on Connecticut's Gold Coast, where she could curl up in a forgotten corner and escape into her books.

Her mother was the more approachable of her parents, but only if Kendra conformed to her precise specifications of what a debutante should be in the time-honored fashion of most of *her* family, who proudly traced their lineage to the *Mayflower*. To please her, Kendra had attended Mount Holyoke like every other woman in her family since the college was founded, but as she grew older she'd come to understand that the only way to gain her father's attention was to try to take part in the only thing that mattered to him, his business.

She wished she hadn't now.

The clock kept ticking, and Kendra had no desire to explain why she was dragging her feet to the Skalas security team, who had already thoroughly searched her car and her person and had sent her photograph up to the executive floor. Where, she had been told coldly, she was expected. Within ten minutes or she would be deemed a security risk.

Kendra forced herself to get out of the car and shivered, though it wasn't cold. She didn't like New York City, that was all. It was too loud, too chaotic, *too much*. Even here, several stories beneath ground with the famous Skalas Tower slicing into the sky above her, an architectural marvel of steel and glass, she was certain she could feel the weight of so many *lives* streaming about on the streets. On top of her.

Or, possibly, that was her trepidation talking.

Because she'd been so sure she would never, ever have to come face-to-face with Balthazar Skalas again.

She smoothed down her pencil skirt, but didn't give in to the urge to jump back in the car and check her carefully minimal makeup for the nineteenth time. There was no point.

This was happening, and she *would* face him and the truth was, she was likely flattering herself to think that he would even recognize her.

The flutter low in her belly suggested that it was not so simple as mere *flattery,* but Kendra ignored that as she marched across the concrete toward the bank of elevators, clearly marked and unavoidable.

It had been years, after all. And this was an office building, however exquisite, not one of her family's self-conscious parties packed full of the rich and the powerful, where Kendra was expected to present herself as her mother's pride and her father's indulgence. Such gatherings were the only reason she'd ever met or mingled with the kinds of people her father and brother admired so much, like Balthazar Skalas himself—feared and worshipped in turn by all and sundry.

Because Thomas certainly had no interest in letting Kendra work alongside him in the company.

Tommy had always laughed at her ambitions. She'd love to think, now, that he'd wanted to keep her at bay because she'd have discovered what he was up to sooner. But she knew the truth of that, too. Tommy didn't think of her at all. And was certainly not threatened by anything she might or might not do, as he'd made clear today in no uncertain terms.

A reasonable person might ask herself why, when her father and brother had always acted as if she was an interloper as well as an afterthought—and her mother cared about her but only in between her garden parties and charity events—Kendra was carrying out this unpleasant task for them.

That was the trouble.

It was the *only* task she'd ever been asked to perform for them.

She couldn't help thinking it was therefore her only chance to prove herself. To prove that she was worthy of being a Connolly. That she was more than an afterthought. That she deserved to take her place in the company, be more than her mother's occasional dress up doll, and who knew? Maybe get treated, at last, like she was one of them.

And maybe if that happened she wouldn't

feel so lonely, for once. Maybe if she showed them how useful she was, she wouldn't feel so excluded by her family, the way she always had.

No matter how many times she told herself it was simply because she was so much younger than her brother, or because she represented a strange moment in her parents' otherwise distant marriage, it stung that she was always so easily dismissed. So easily ignored, left out, or simply not told about the various issues that affected all of them.

Maybe this time she could show them that she belonged.

So even though the very idea of what she might have to do made her stomach a heavy lead ball, and even though she thought Tommy would be better off accepting whatever punishment came his way for his behavior—for once—she marched herself to the elevator marked *Executive Level*, put in the code she'd been given, and stepped briskly inside when the doors slid soundlessly open before her.

That her heart began to catapult around inside her chest was neither here nor there.

"I don't understand why you think a man as powerful and ruthless as Balthazar Skalas will listen to me," she'd told her father, sitting there in the uncomfortable chair on the other side of his desk. She had not said, *My own father doesn't listen to me, why should he?* "Surely he'd be more likely to listen to you."

Thomas had given a bitter laugh. He'd actually looked at her directly, without that patronizing glaze that usually took him over in her presence. "Balthazar Skalas has washed his hands of the Connolly Company. As far as he's concerned, I am as guilty as Tommy."

A traitorous part of Kendra had almost cheered at that, because surely that would encourage her father to finally face the truth about his son. But she knew better.

"All the more reason to want nothing to do with me, I would have thought," she'd said instead. "As I, too, am a Connolly."

"Kendra. Please. You have nothing to do with the company." Thomas Connolly had waved one of his hands in a dismissive sort of way, as if Kendra's dreams were that silly. "You must appeal to him as…a family man."

Her head had been alive with those too-bright, too-hot images of Balthazar Skalas she carried around inside and tried to hide, even from herself. Especially from herself. Because he was... Excessive. Too dangerous. Too imperious. Too arrogantly beautiful. Even his name conjured up the kind of devil he was.

But it didn't do any justice to the reality of him, that cruel mouth and eyes like the darkest hellfire. And oh, how he could make the unwary burn...

She'd flushed, but luckily her father paid little attention to such inconsequential things as his only daughter's demeanor or emotional state. This was the first time he'd ever wanted more from her than a pretty smile, usually aimed at his lecherous business associates at a party.

"What does he know of family?" Kendra had been proud of herself for sounding much calmer than she felt, though it had taken an act of will to keep from pressing her palms to her hot cheeks. "I thought he and that brother of his were engaged in some kind of civil war."

"*He* can be at war with his brother, but I do not suggest anyone else attempt it. They are still running the same company."

"I'm sure I read an article that claimed they'd balkanized the corporation so that each one of them need not—"

"Then you must appeal to him as a man, Kendra," her father had said, very distinctly.

And they'd stared at each other, across the width of that grand desk of his that he claimed some ancestor or another had won from Andrew Carnegie in a wager. Kendra told herself she must have misheard him. Or misunderstood it. Her heart had been pounding so hard that she felt it everywhere. Her temples. Her wrists. Beneath her collarbone.

Somehow she had kept her composure.

But in case she'd had any doubt about what her father might have meant by that, Tommy had waylaid her moments after she'd left her father's study. She'd rounded the corner and he'd been there, flashing that grin of his that always meant he thought he was being charming.

Kendra knew better. She hadn't found him charming in as long as she could remember. Ever, even. A side effect of knowing him, she would have said.

Not that anyone had ever asked her.

"Don't tell me you're wearing that," he'd growled at her, a contemptuous glare raking her from head to toe. "You look like a secretary. Not really what we're going for here."

"No need to thank me for running off to rescue you," Kendra had replied tartly. "The sacrifice is its own reward."

Tommy had grabbed her arm, hard. Deliberately hard, she'd assumed, but she'd learned a long time ago never to show him any weakness.

"I don't know what Dad told you," he snarled at her. "But there's only one way out of this. We have to make sure that Skalas won't try to press charges against me. And that's not going to happen with you in this dowdy, forgettable outfit."

"I'm going to appeal to his sense of family,

Tommy." She'd ignored his comments about her outfit because there was no point arguing with him. He always went low and mean. Always.

Tommy had laughed. In a way that had sent cold water rushing down her spine in a torrent. "Balthazar Skalas hates his family. He's not looking for a trip down memory lane, sis. But rumor is, he's always looking for a new mistress."

"You can't mean…"

Her brother had shaken his head. Then her, too, because he was still gripping her arm. "You have one chance to prove you're not useless, Kendra. If I were you, I wouldn't waste it."

Hours later, she was still numb. The inside of the executive elevator was sleek and mirrored, and Kendra could *see* the panic on her own face, mixed right in with the smattering of freckles her mother abhorred. She wanted, more than anything, to pretend her father had meant something different. That Tommy was just being Tommy.

But she knew better.

That sinking feeling inside told her so.

What's the difference, really? she asked herself as the elevator shot up. *A mistress or a loveless marriage?*

Because Tommy might have asked her to make herself a mistress, but her mother had been trying to marry Kendra off for years. Emily Cabot Connelly hadn't understood why Kendra hadn't graduated from college with an engagement ring. And she'd taken a dim view of Kendra's attempts over the past three years to convince Thomas to give her a job at the company when that was no way to find an appropriate husband.

"I don't want *to get married,"* Kendra had protested the last time the topic had come up, a few weeks ago on the way to a dreary tea party for some or other pet charity of Emily's.

"Darling, no one wants *to get married. You have certain responsibilities due to your station in life. And certain compensations for the choices that must result."* Her mother had laughed. *"What does* want *have to do with anything?"*

Kendra knew her mother expected her to

do as she had done. Marry to consolidate assets, then live a life of leisure as a reward that she could make meaningful in whatever way suited her. Charities. Foundations. If she wanted, she could even hare off to the Continent like her black sheep of a great-aunt and "forget" to come home again.

If she thought about it that way, Kendra supposed becoming a mistress to a man like Balthazar Skalas would be much the same thing, if of shorter duration.

The reward was the point, not the relationship.

No one seemed to care that Kendra wanted to make her own reward.

The elevator rose so fast the leaden ball that was her stomach stayed behind, buried beneath the ground. She saw a security camera with its red light blinking at her from one corner and was happy that it was there. It reminded her to remain composed. She was here for a business meeting, in sensible heels with her pencil skirt and a dark, silky blouse that made her feel like the vice president of the family business that she intended to become one day.

I do not look like a secretary, she told herself, eyeing her reflection.

But she also did not look like a woman auditioning to be the mistress of a man like Balthazar Skalas.

A man she kept assuring herself would not remember her. He must attend a thousand parties, and if that flash of heat that sometimes woke her in the night was any guide, affected at least a thousand women in precisely the same way.

As she watched, her cheeks grew red.

It didn't matter what her father or Tommy said, because she was the one who had to do this thing. And she had to believe that a cool, measured approach, neither denying Tommy's transgressions nor attempting to find a better side to a man who she already knew had only hard edges, was a reasonable course of action.

Unless he remembers you, a treacherous voice inside her whispered.

When the elevator doors opened again,

she walked out briskly. And if she'd been in any doubt as to where she was, the lobby she found herself in reminded her. It was all sleek marble with the company name etched into stone. *Skalas & Sons*. Almost as if theirs was a quaint little family enterprise, when, in fact, the late Demetrius Skalas had been the richest man on earth at one time.

When he died, his two sons had taken the reins of the multinational corporation that sprawled about into different industries. Everyone had predicted they would run the business into the ground. Instead, the two of them had doubled their father's wealth within the first two years of their ownership. Each one of them was now far richer than their father had ever been.

Something no article she'd ever read about the Skalas family—and she'd read them all— failed to trumpet.

Balthazar was the eldest son. He split his time between the company's headquarters in Athens and important satellite offices like this one and was considered the more serious of the two brothers. Constantine was the flashier of the two, thanks to his penchant for race cars and models, and he spent more time in the London office.

The rumor was they detested each other.

But neither Skalas brother ever responded to rumors about their personal lives.

Kendra had expected the office to be empty as it was coming up on eight o'clock that night—the only time the great Balthazar had found in his tightly packed schedule. Instead, she could hear the hum of activity, and as she walked toward the reception area, could see people hurrying back and forth as if it was eight in the morning.

The woman waiting behind the reception desk offered a perfunctory smile. "Ms. Connolly, I trust?" When Kendra nodded, because she seemed to have lost her voice somewhere on the trip from her car, the woman pressed a few buttons. "Mr. Skalas is on a call, but will be with you shortly."

She stood and led Kendra through the great glass doors behind her desk into the rest of the office. Then walked briskly on heels that were not the least bit sensible, making it look as if she was gliding on air.

It made Kendra instantly feel inadequate.

Still, there was nothing to do but follow the woman where she led. Instead of turning toward the noise and people, the receptionist took her in the other direction. Where there was only a long, gleaming, marble hallway with one side dedicated to an art collection so fine it made Kendra's head spin. On the other side, floor-to-ceiling windows showed Manhattan laid out at her feet. She couldn't help but feel as if she was walking along the ramparts of an ancient castle, forced to sacrifice herself before a terrible king for the good of her village—

But imagining that she was in the Dark Ages didn't make this any better.

At the end of the hall the receptionist led her into another room, this one clearly also a waiting area, but far more elegant. And hushed.

"This is Mr. Skalas's private waiting area," the woman told her. "Please make yourself comfortable. If you require assistance, you may step across the hall, where the secretarial staff will be happy to help in any way they can."

Then she was gone.

Leaving Kendra alone with her mounting panic.

She couldn't bear to sit, afraid she might come out of her own skin. She stood and stared out the windows instead.

"There's nothing to fear," she told herself firmly, if under her breath. "He won't remember anything about you."

The real trouble was that *she* remembered all too well.

She didn't recall what charity event her mother had used as an excuse that summer. Kendra had only just graduated from Mount Holyoke, certain it would be a matter of months before she could take her rightful place in the family company. She'd figured it was her job, then, to act the part of the businessperson she intended to become. She might not have taken naturally to the world of business—far preferring a good book and a quiet place to read it to the endless rounds of deals and drinks and men in their golf togs—but who ever said life was about what *felt* good? Surely it was about what a person did, not what they dreamed about. Accordingly, she'd been putting herself out there. She might not have *felt* sparkling and effervescent, the way her mother always told her she ought to, but she could pretend.

And so she had, waving a cocktail around as she'd laughed and mingled and exhausted herself so thoroughly that after dinner, she'd sneaked off for a few moments' break. The dancing was about to begin beneath the grand tent that sprawled over the part of her parents' lawn that offered the best views of Long Island Sound.

She paid no mind to the distraught woman who passed her in a rush of tears and silk on the trellis path that led to her favorite gazebo, set up above the rocky shoreline. It was a pretty evening and the air was warm with scents of salt, grass, and flowers. She could hear the band playing behind her as she walked, and she welcomed the dim light of the evenly spaced lanterns along her way because they were far less intrusive than the brightness inside the tent. She could drop her smile. She could breathe.

It was only when she climbed the steps to the gazebo that she saw him standing against the far rail, almost lost in the shadows.

And then wondered how she could possibly not have *felt* his presence, so intense was he. The *punch* of him.

Kendra had felt winded.

He wore a dark suit that should have made him indistinguishable from every other man at that party. But instead she found herself stunned by the width of his shoulders, his offhanded athletic grace. His mouth was a stern line, his eyes deep set and thunderous. His hair was thick and dark and looked as if he had been running his fingers through it— though it occurred to her, with a jolt, that it had probably not been *his* fingers.

It had been a clear, bright evening, but she suddenly felt as if a summer storm had rolled in off the Sound. As if the clouds were thick and low. Threatening.

And all he did was lift a brow, arrogant and

ruthless at once. "I don't believe I sent for a replacement."

It had made no sense. Later, she would tell herself it was something about the way he'd gazed at her as if he'd brought her into being. She'd never seen anything like it before. All that fire. All that warning. And other things she couldn't define.

He'd lifted two fingers and beckoned her near.

It hadn't occurred to her to disobey. Kendra drifted closer, aware of herself in a way she never had been before. Her breasts felt thick and heavy in the bodice of her dress when she usually forgot they were there. Her thighs seemed to brush against each other, rich whispers. And between her legs, she felt herself heat, then melt.

But this spellbinding man gazed at her in stark command, and she could do nothing at all but go to him.

"So eager," he murmured when she drew near.

Kendra hadn't known what that meant, either. His words didn't make any sense, and yet the sound of them soared inside of her. She felt as if she was a fluttering, desperate, small thing that he could easily hold in the palm of his hand—

Then he did.

He wrapped a hand around the nape of her neck and hauled her those last few, thrilling inches toward him. She found her hands on his chest and the sheer heat of him seemed to wallop her, making her knees go weak.

"Very well," he'd said. "You'll do."

Then he'd set his mouth to her neck.

And Kendra had died.

There was no other explanation for what happened to her. His mouth against her skin, toying with her, tasting her. She felt her mouth open wide as if on a silent scream, but all she did was let her head fall back in delicious, delirious surrender.

The hand that gripped her neck dropped like a band of steel around her hips, drawing her even harder against him.

It was too much. She could hear the sound of the party in the distance, laughter and the clinking of glasses, but she was *on fire*.

And then she felt his hand move beneath the hem of her dress, volcanic and impossible.

She didn't like to remember any of this. It had been three years and it was as if it had only just happened. She could feel everything as if it was happening now, high above Manhattan with her hands pressed to the glass that was all that separated her from stepping out into air.

A fall that seemed tame in comparison to Balthazar Skalas in a darkened gazebo on a summer night.

She had opened her mouth again, that time to stop the madness—or so she liked to tell herself now—but nothing came out. His mouth continued to toy with her skin, chasing fire along her clavicle and sucking gently on the pulse at the base of her neck.

And meanwhile, his hand, huge and utterly without hesitation, skimmed its way up the inside of one thigh to the edge of her panties. Then, before she could even find the words to protest—or encourage him, more like— he stroked his way beneath.

Her whole life, Kendra had considered herself remarkably self-possessed. It came from being raised like an only child, so much younger was she than her brother. Always in the company of adults. Always expected to act far older than she was. Her friends in boarding school and college had always allowed impetuousness to lead them down questionable roads, but never Kendra. Never.

But that night, none of that mattered.

Because Balthazar stroked his way into her melting heat, and Kendra...disappeared.

There was only that strong arm at her back, his mouth on her neck, his fingers between her legs as he played with her. He murmured something she didn't understand, rough and low against the tender skin in the crook of her neck, that only later it would occur to her was likely Greek.

But she didn't have to understand the words to know that whatever he said, it was filthy.

It had shot through her like a lightning bolt.

She'd made a noise then, a sob, and he'd growled something in reply. And then he'd pinched her. Not hard, but not gently, either. That proud little peak that already throbbed—

Kendra had bucked against him, lost and wild and heaving out another kind of sob, high-pitched and keening.

How had the whole of the East Coast not heard her?

When she finally stopped shaking, she'd found him staring down at her, a kind of thunder on that face of his, so harsh that it was almost sensual. Brutally masculine and connected, somehow, to all the places where she'd still quivered. To where his hand still cupped her, so that all her molten heat was flooding his hand.

A notion that made another shudder rip through her.

"You are surprising," he'd said, rough and low. "I am not usually surprised. Come."

He'd pulled his hand from her panties, and she'd thought that harsh line of his mouth almost curved when she'd swayed, unable to stand on her own once he released her.

"Come?" she repeated.

"You're more of a meal than a snack," he had told her then, too much heat in his dark gaze. "And I prefer to savor my meals. I have a house not far from here."

Reality had reasserted itself with a sickening thud. What on earth did she think she was doing?

A question she still couldn't answer, three years later.

The back of her neck prickled then. She sucked in a breath as she turned, then froze.

It was as if she'd summoned him. He stood in a door she hadn't known was there, that must have opened soundlessly, because she had no idea how long he had been watching her.

He was just as she remembered. Balthazar Skalas, the devil himself, his deep dark eyes alive with mockery and that cruel twist to his mouth.

And she could tell, instantly, that he remembered her perfectly.

"Kendra Connolly," he said, as if he was tasting her name. His dark eyes glittered and she felt it. Everywhere. "Your brazenness is astonishing, truly. Have you finally come to finish what you started?"

CHAPTER TWO

BALTHAZAR SKALAS DETESTED the Connolly family.

He had long despised Thomas Connolly, who considered himself far more charismatic than he was and acted as if that supposed charisma made him a force to be reckoned with. When the only thing it had truly made him was appealing to the vulnerable and therefore a sworn enemy to Balthazar and his brother. His son had always been useless at best and otherwise wholly laughable.

Balthazar had been waiting for the time to deal with the elder Connolly for years. He might have forgiven the younger's nonsense—or at least ignored it, the way he did all things beneath his notice—had foolish Tommy Connolly not believed he could steal from Balthazar with impunity.

In the grand scheme of things, overcharging Skalas & Sons and pocketing the difference mattered little to Balthazar. It was the principle that offended him. It was the noxious Tommy Connolly's clear belief that he *could* cheat Balthazar that he could not allow.

Still, he could admit that sending the daughter to handle her family's sins was an inspired choice. He would have refused to see the father or the son.

"I was certain my secretarial staff was mistaken when they told me you kept calling." He watched her closely as she stood there, framed by the gleaming city behind her, yet seeming to glow the brighter. "Begging for an appointment when, last I saw you, you were far more interested in running away."

Kendra had fooled him back then, when no one fooled him. *Him.* And in the privacy of his own mind, he could admit that it had been more than her brother's theft that had made him detest her family. That her brother's behavior had merely confirmed what he had already concluded. Because of that night long ago, with her.

Balthazar was not accustomed to wanting things he could not have.

Instantly.

"I'm here on behalf of my family," Kendra Connolly said, her voice cool. Something like professional, when he could see the heat he remembered on her cheeks and in her gleaming, golden eyes.

A liar, then. He should not have felt even the faintest inkling of surprise.

Much less something that veered a little too close to disappointment for his taste.

"They consider you the most appropriate weapon, do they?" he asked smoothly. "I think your family is misreading this situation."

She blinked at that, but didn't collapse. Or shrink in on herself. Both reactions he'd seen in puffed-up male CEOs who stood before him and risked his displeasure.

Unlike them, Kendra…bothered him. Balthazar could remember too well the heat of her in his hand—though he still couldn't understand why she should affect him so. When women blurred in his recollection, becoming one grand and glorious smear of sensation and release. Yet he could recall her taste in his mouth. The silk of her skin.

The way she'd come fully in his grip.

To say that Balthazar resented that was a vast understatement.

"I appreciate you seeing me," Kendra said in the same collected way, folding her hands before her in a manner that might have seemed polite and calm had he not also seen the evidence that she was gripping her own fingers much too hard. Why did he find that…soothing? "I'm not here to excuse my brother's actions."

"I should hope not. He stole. From *me*. And worse still, believed that he could get away with it." He smiled. Thinly. "It is the arrogance I cannot abide."

He had tasted that pulse in her neck. Perhaps that was why he could not seem to look away from it now. Particularly not when he could see how hard and wild it beat.

He blamed her for that, too.

"I don't expect you to forgive him. Or even think kindly on him. Why would you?"

"Why, indeed?"

"What I'm hoping is that you and I can come to some kind of agreement. If there's a way that I might convince you that notifying the authorities isn't necessary, I would love to find it."

Balthazar laughed at that, though there was little mirth in it. He pushed himself away from the doorjamb and made his way into his actual office, a sprawling affair that shouted out his wealth and consequence from every possible angle. There were walls of glass on two sides, making it seem as if they floated over Manhattan. Steel and granite everywhere, gleaming as much with quiet menace as with wealth.

He liked to announce who he was. So there could be no mistake.

When he rounded the great slab that served as his desk, he was not surprised to find that Kendra had trailed after him and now stood uncertainly just inside the door.

"What on earth makes you think that I would do such a thing?" he asked her, genuinely interested in her answer. "The sheer hubris of it. The unmitigated gall. You must rate yourself highly indeed if you imagine you can convince me of…anything."

She spread her hands out in front of her, a gesture of surrender. It should not have made him so greedy for a taste of her, surely. "I'm not going to pretend to you that my brother Tommy isn't problematic."

"You are here anyway. Sent to defend him. Yet what defense can you possibly mount for a creature so reckless and self-destructive?"

"None."

That surprised him, when he prided himself on never allowing business machinations to surprise him. He stood behind his desk, one finger on the granite surface, and it was only when he realized he was tapping it that he understood he was more agitated than he allowed himself to appear in public.

Balthazar added that to the long list of things he blamed on this woman.

"You did not come here to mount a defense for his sins?"

"What defense could there be?" Kendra asked quietly. "I know my brother's weaknesses better than you, I assure you. While I cannot imagine why he should find it necessary to fudge the books when he already has more than enough money of his own, it's clear to me that he did. Even my father, always Tommy's greatest defender, had nothing to say to help this make any sense. Tommy himself offered no explanation."

"Of course not. Greed is really quite simple, *kopéla*. He wanted more. So he took it."

"I'm not going to pretend to you that I understand every detail of the accounting here." She lifted her chin, but kept her gaze steady on his, when men twice her size would quail before him. "I understand stealing, however. I'm prepared to pay you back, with interest. Today."

"And again, you misunderstand." He smiled then, noting the way she flinched, then tried to hide it. "I don't want your money. I want your ruin."

Or her father's shame, but that would come. Her cheeks had been bright since she'd followed him into the room, but she paled then.

"My understanding is that it added up to

two and a half million, give or take. A good chunk of change, I grant you. My father intends to pay it back from his personal account. In cash, if necessary. And there should be no cause for financial ruin."

Balthazar had spent some time imagining this moment. He relished it.

"You mistake me," he said quietly. Distinctly. "I am not speaking of money. It is your family I wish to see ruined, Kendra. Your father and his arrogance in particular. You and I both know perfectly well that your family would be tarnished forever if I dragged your brother through the courts. No one would be surprised, mind you, only distinctly horrified in that particular old money way that your Tommy was caught. And I believe the rest of your family might find themselves...less welcome in the circles you all currently enjoy."

And he would count that a decent start.

She looked distressed for the first time since she'd appeared in his waiting room, and he'd expected that to feel like more of a triumph than it did. "There must be some way I can convince you that you don't need to do that."

Balthazar studied her. "What do you have that you think I might want?"

Something in him swelled then, bitter and almost furious, as Kendra swallowed. Hard. Then started toward him with determination stamped all over her face.

If she'd put up a sign advertising her wares on a street corner, she could not have been more obvious.

And he'd expected this, hadn't he? It confirmed what he'd already suspected. That three years ago, she'd been sent out to that gazebo to see how far she could get with him.

To tempt, then tease.

It had Thomas Connolly's hands all over it. And damn the man, damn his unforgivable arrogance, but he had succeeded.

Balthazar would rather die where he stood than admit *how* successful Thomas Connolly had actually been.

Because at first he hadn't known who she was. He had stood there longer than he cared to remember after she'd left, trying to understand what had occurred. He could not recall the last time a woman had *fled* from him. Because it had never happened.

Women tend to run toward him, not away.

He had been irritated, courtesy of Isabella, the mistress he'd finished with only moments before Kendra had found him there in the gazebo. And not because any of the insults or accusations Isabella had flung at him had landed. Much less held any weight. He had never cared for her emotional outbursts and had paid them little mind throughout the six months of their arrangement.

But he liked his sex regular and often. Knowing that, Isabella had deliberately forced their conversation that night, well aware that he'd been aching for release.

Isabella might have cried as she'd stormed away from him, but he knew the tears were more for the loss of her access to her allowance than any true emotion. Just as he knew that the moment she stepped back into the light of the party, the tears would miraculously dry up, she would take deep pleasure in having left him unsatisfied and she would begin scouting for a new benefactor.

He had sent an abrupt message to his assistant to cut Isabella off and then had stood there, annoyed.

But then Kendra had appeared.

He hadn't known who she was and so to him, Kendra had seemed like a breath of fresh air after Isabella's sultry, cloying, obviousness.

Those soft, rosy cheeks. The hint of freckles across her nose, when he would have sworn no imperfections were permitted in these hallowed halls of the so-called American elite. Her hair had been swept up into something elegant, though tendrils fell down, and the red in it had shone like flame in the soft light from the lanterns outside the gazebo.

She had stopped before him like a startled fawn, her gleaming eyes wide, her sensual lips parted.

Balthazar did not believe in innocence. And yet that night, he had been tempted to imagine she might be the exception that proved the rule.

She had proved him wrong in short order.

No innocent could possibly melt like that, arching back beneath the onslaught of his need, his longing, both pounding through him like a storm. No innocent would open herself up to him so eagerly, then come apart in his palm so readily.

He'd been so hard he'd ached, another new sensation. He'd wanted to peel her out of the dress she wore, lay her out beneath him on a wide bed in a room with a locked door and sate himself fully.

Instead she had turned away, then run.

And when he'd finally made his way back into the tedious party, astounded at what had happened to him, everything had made a sickening kind of sense.

Thomas Connolly, the pompous git, had been making a speech with his family arrayed behind him. Smirking Tommy, the sort of vicious alcoholic heir who thought his money would protect him from his sins. The overtly medicated wife, looking blank and distant even up close.

And Kendra, the daughter, Balthazar understood in that instant was as corrupt as the rest of them, for all she had stood beside her mother, reeking of the innocence he knew she did not possess.

Eighteen months later, when the first discrepancies in Skalas & Sons' accounts with the Connolly family's shipping concern appeared, Balthazar could have made his move. But he had remembered that night, the sheer heat of Kendra in his hand, and had waited.

He had not merely allowed Tommy his rope. He had spooled it out himself so there could be no doubt whatsoever when Tommy hung himself with it.

Balthazar told himself it was triumph, not disappointment, that pounded in him as Kendra came to stand just there on the other side of his desk.

Because he should have known that night three years ago that she was like the rest of her family, whether he'd known who she was or not. That he'd been fooled for even a moment gnawed at him.

There was no such thing as innocence. Not in his world and certainly not in her morally bankrupt family. For his part, Balthazar had been raised a Skalas, which was akin to walking forth with a golden target on his back. He had never had a single friend—or woman, or colleague—who had not betrayed him, or could be prevailed upon to betray him, for the right price.

A lesson he had learned young.

His own brother would cheerfully stab him in the back if it benefited him. Balthazar had no doubt about that. It was why he and Constantine had split things up neatly between them. Better not to offer each other the temptation, they'd decided.

The threat of mutually assured destruction kept them friendly enough, no matter what the tabloids said. They were the only thing they had, after all.

Something that was certainly not true of Kendra Connolly.

"What exactly are you offering me?" he asked her, trying to keep his tone even when inside, he raged.

She was close enough now that he could read her expression. Or try. He could have sworn what he saw there was something like misery. Or apprehension.

Or, a cynical voice inside him chimed in, *she's merely good at what she does.*

Too good.

Because he was certain, for a moment, that he could detect a faint tremor in her lips. Before she firmed them into a straight line and he became equally certain he'd imagined it.

"Name your price," she invited him.

"I am more interested in what it is you think I want." He eyed her as he would any conquest, business or personal. Assessing profit and loss. Looking for weaknesses to exploit to his benefit. "What can you imagine you have to offer that I do not already have?"

She spread out her hands again, though this time it read as less of a surrender.

"Me," she said.

Balthazar watched that pulse in her neck react. If he didn't know better, he would think that she was desperate when he felt certain that she was not. That this, like that night three years ago, was nothing but more deception.

"I think you overestimate your charms," he said with cruel deliberation. "Do you really imagine you are worth more than two million dollars?"

She blanched at that, but stood her ground. "Of course."

"I do not wish to insult you," he murmured. Though that was a lie. "But I would not pay a single dollar for something I could get for free. In abundance. And do."

"And here I thought you preferred to keep mistresses," she shot back at him, to his great surprise. "Hardly free, is it?"

"You should be less opaque." Balthazar shrugged. "One night to clear your brother's debt? That is not so appealing. But a mistress? Mine for as long as I am interested? That is a different proposition altogether. Though far more...strenuous."

Her lips were pressed tight together. If he was not mistaken, her hands had started to curl into fists before she dropped them to her sides.

"Marvelous," she said with a certain brightness he could see was false. As she, herself, was false, no matter his body's response. "Is that what you want?"

"Normally I am the one who makes this offer." He smirked. "It is not pressed upon me by a woman desperate to clear the name of a brother she would be better off disowning."

"Families are complicated."

"I thought my family was complicated. I am forever reading fables the media has created to explain things between my brother or myself. Or tales of my late father." He studied her, then affected a measure of outraged astonishment. "But I will confess, when I granted you this appointment, I never expected *this*."

Her chin lifted higher. "What did you expect?"

"Excuses." He eyed her until she flushed. "What a martyr you are, Kendra."

Her eyes, that intriguing shade of amber that sometimes looked like gold, glittered. "I would never call myself a martyr."

"Oh, no? And yet here you are. Sacrificing yourself." He laughed when all she did was glare at him. "You do not understand how this works, do you? You're supposed to at least *act* as if you're motivated by uncontrollable lust, whatever your true motivations."

"Tell me what you need," Kendra implored him, her voice tight. "There's no need to play all these games, is there?"

"But perhaps what I want from you is the game."

She looked away then, her throat working. "Very well then."

"But how will we come to terms?" Balthazar mused, and stopped pretending he wasn't fully enjoying himself. "There are so many considerations. You will not need my financial support, clearly, as you will be paying off a debt. I will require full access, of course, but that is easy enough. I have any number of properties that will suit."

"Access," she echoed. "Full access."

He laughed. "What is it you think a mistress does?"

She cleared her throat, still looking away. "To be honest, I thought it was a silly, archaic word to describe a rich man's relationships."

"You can call it a relationship if you like. In

truth, it is a business arrangement. I find it is better to spell out any and all expectations in advance, the better to avoid unpleasant mis-understandings." He shrugged again, expansively. "I want what I want. When I want it."

To her credit, she turned back and met his gaze. "By which, you mean sex."

"Sex, yes. And anything else I desire." He laughed at the expression on her face. The one she tried to hide. "That could mean accompaniment. The ability to charm business associates at tedious dinners. Clever conversation, sparkling repartee, and all while looking like a bauble most men cannot afford. But if I were you, Kendra, I would focus more on the sex. I require rather a lot."

He was fascinated by the way her expression changed, then. By the way the color on her face matched. If he didn't know better—if he didn't know to his detriment that she was a loaded, aimed weapon—he might have been tempted to think she was doing this against her will. Or if not precisely against her will, without the level of enthusiasm he would have anticipated from an operator like her. Like all the members of her family.

Because surely she had done things like this before or why would they have sent her?

You know she's done things like this before, he reminded himself sharply. *She's done it to you.*

"Are you prepared?" she asked him after a moment, and though her voice was slightly husky, there was no hint of uncertainty about her. She was hiding it well—another indication this was a role she was playing. "If you take me as your mistress, you will be linked with my family. In a way I'm guessing you will not like."

"I do not think that I am the one who will dislike it most."

"You and I can stand here and speak of a business arrangement, but I think you know the tabloids will assume that it's a more conventional relationship."

"If the tabloids did not make assumptions, they would not exist." He made a dismissive gesture. "This is of no interest to me."

"All right then." She squared her shoulders as if prepared to march forth into battle. "How do these things normally begin?"

He might have admired her bravado had it not been predicated on how little she actually wanted him. And how little she was attempting to hide that fact from him.

"I have not invited you to be my mistress, Kendra," he rebuked her. Mildly enough. "This discussion, while illuminating, is nothing more than academic."

"What do you mean, academic?" Color flooded her cheeks again, and he found himself far more interested than he ought to have been. Fascinated, even, despite himself. "I'm offering myself to you."

"But you cannot be trusted." He shook his head sadly. "You are a Connolly, first of all, and by definition a liar. More importantly, you have already attempted to lure me in once."

"You thought I was attempting to…" When Kendra shook her head it was as if she couldn't quite get her balance. She blinked. "My mistake. You're apparently playing strange games.

If you did not wish to do business, you should have said so."

"I admire a woman who can barter. Particularly when what she is bartering is herself. No coy games. No fluttering about like all the rest, never quite getting to the mercenary point."

Her eyes flashed. "If you're not interested in the business arrangement you suggested, tell me what would interest you instead."

Balthazar was intrigued, and that should have worried him when he knew her to be an empty, grasping liar, like all the rest of her family. She was treacherous and as dirty as the rest of them. But he could not deny that he was hard. That he ached for her.

There was only one way to soothe that kind of ache, no matter what manner of woman inspired it.

"This particular kind of business arrangement requires, shall we say, a down payment," he told her. Matter-of-factly.

"A down payment. On sex."

"But of course. I prefer my sex—"

"Abundant," she clipped out. "I heard you."

"Abundant, yes. But I also require a certain level of excellence, or what would be the point?" He smiled at her, edgily. "All I know about you is that you are selfish. And a tease. And entirely too willing to do your family's bidding. None of that, I must say, suggests to me that you would be any good at all in the bedroom."

He thought he heard a sharp sound, like an intake of breath.

"Am I to understand, then…?" Her eyes had gone a brilliant shade of bright amber, but her voice was precise. Crisp and to the point. "That is to say, I assume what you're asking for is an audition?"

"We're talking about more than two million dollars, Kendra," he said with no little dark amusement. "I need to be certain I am getting my money's worth. You understand."

He expected her to turn and run from the room, screaming perhaps. No matter how many times she'd attempted to vamp her way out of trouble—a notion he could not say he enjoyed entertaining, though he shoved it aside—he doubted very much that anyone had ever spoken to her quite like this.

All those preppy, pastel-wearing country club scions of this or that supposedly elite family, as if there was such a thing in this adolescent country. All those Ivy League boys. All this American nonsense so many millennia after his own country had taken shape and changed the world.

It was something, all these pretensions to aristocracy. It really was. Balthazar could never tell if he admired these brash people or pitied them.

Still, he didn't like imagining any of them with Kendra.

And if there was something in him that regretted what he planned to do here—what he should have been *delighted* to do here—he shoved it aside.

But to his surprise, she only shrugged in return. "That sounds fair." Her voice was so nonchalant it poked at him. She arched an elegant brow. "Right here?"

He felt that like a shot of electricity, straight to his sex. When he should have felt nothing of the kind. When he had anticipated feeling only the sweetness of his long overdue revenge. And had perhaps imagined she would run from him again.

Still, he did not back down. He was Balthazar Skalas. Backing down was not in his blood—his father had seen to that by spilling it himself, long ago. More, he had vowed that he would wipe the Connolly family off the map, one by one.

And so he would, starting now.

"Right here is fine, Kendra." He inclined his head. "You can begin by stripping."

CHAPTER THREE

KENDRA KEPT WAITING for the floor to open up and swallow her whole. But it did not.

The situation had gone from terrible to outrageous to something far worse, and she wanted nothing more than to run away. But she couldn't.

Because this was Tommy's only chance. She might not think much of Tommy and his endless messes, but she knew that Balthazar was right. If he dragged her brother through court, it would kill her parents.

And Kendra might think that her father could use a little humbling, sure. It certainly wouldn't do him any harm. But she didn't think her mother deserved the same. After all, what had Emily ever done but what she was expected to do? Did she truly deserve the scorn of all the women who'd made the same choices she had—because that was what she would get, in spades.

It didn't seem fair that Emily should bear the brunt of Tommy's poor decisions.

Honestly, it didn't seem fair that Kendra should, either.

But she'd wanted to do this, hadn't she? Wanted to help, anyway, even if she hadn't wanted *this*, precisely…

Liar, a voice inside chided her. *You want whatever you can get.*

Because what little she'd gotten from him had been haunting her for years.

Why was that so hard to admit?

She told herself to calm down. To get a hold of herself. Yes, Balthazar was every bit as awful—and if she dared admit it to herself, as exciting—as she remembered. He was like a force of nature. Overwhelming and electric and impossible to look away from. The idea of actually *having sex* with this man made her feel hollowed out with the heat of it.

Kendra wasn't sure she'd survive.

Oh, come on, she chided herself. *How hard can it really be to do what he's asking you to do? People do it all the time. The world is filled with people doing it* right this minute.

Maybe not bargaining to be the mistress of a man who was essentially a stranger, but the sex part, certainly. Kendra bet if she went and looked out the vast windows at the other lit up buildings, she would see people doing all kinds of things in those anonymous squares of light. That was what big cities were for, surely.

She cleared her throat and wished she could clear her head as easily. "To clarify, you want me to get naked, right here in your office. Now."

"Stalling is probably not a good way to begin this arrangement. Or any arrangement, but particularly not one that relies on your naked obedience. Literally."

He sounded amused. More than amused. Those dark eyes of his were glittering, and that cruel mouth of his was set into something not quite a curve. As if he was taking pleasure in this.

In what he was asking her to do.

More, in how desperate she must be if she was really considering *doing* it.

He was a horrible man. The way he spoke about sex and *mistresses* and even her family said absolutely nothing good about his character—

But that wasn't the point, was it? This wasn't about his character.

You don't care about his character, something in her asserted, with a low sort of heat that shook around inside her and made her bones ache.

Because if she wasn't mistaken, what this was really about was how far she was willing to go. Something inside her seemed to soar at that notion.

You don't have to care about what he thinks of you, or what anyone else thinks of you, either, that same voice whispered, hot and deep, making her ache all the more. *You were sent here to do these things.*

In a way, she felt free.

Kendra had always been so afraid of putting a foot wrong, of embarrassing her parents, of causing trouble… But that all seemed to her now to be the dim concerns of a girl she hardly remembered.

Because she was standing before Balthazar Skalas, who wanted her naked.

His dark eyes blazed with how much he wanted it.

She understood, then. He hated her family. She couldn't really blame him for that, of course, given what Tommy had done. But she was a part of that family. Kendra had to assume that he hated her, too.

And she told herself she didn't care about that, but she knew that wasn't true when something in her…hitched.

It didn't matter. She still had to do this.

If only because it was something she alone could do. Neither her father nor Tommy could solve this problem, but she could.

All it took was this.

Free, something within her whispered.

The way she never had been.

"All right, then," she said with as much dignity as she could muster. "If that's what you want."

"Something else you should know about

me," Balthazar said mildly, though that fire in his gaze did not diminish in the slightest, "is that I do not like to repeat myself."

Kendra had the slightly hysterical urge to say something inappropriate. Or perhaps... salute. She bit her tongue. And then, telling herself it was no different from stripping in a doctor's office, started removing her clothes.

Except she didn't.

She ordered herself to move, but her body did not obey. For one jarring thud of her heart. Then another.

All while he stared at her, ruthless and darkly entertained.

Everything seemed to fuse inside of her until she couldn't have said, in that moment, if she was doing this for her family or if she was doing this because Balthazar clearly didn't think she would.

If she stepped back even an inch, she knew it didn't make sense. Getting naked proved nothing at all.

But suddenly it felt as if Kendra's entire life had been leading her to this very moment. As if she needed to prove herself in this bizarre way, or die.

That did it.

She kicked off her shoes. Then, holding his gaze, unfastened the zipper at the back of her skirt, letting it fall to her feet. She stepped out of the circle of fabric and felt that hitch again inside her, because his gaze changed.

The way he looked at her made her think of wild things. Birds of prey, fast and dangerously large cats, predators of every description. There was something impossibly masculine in the way he gazed at her, and it made that place between her legs throb as if his hand was already there, cupping her.

That hard, decidedly male grip, that she'd dreamed about since. Too many times to count.

She pulled off her dark silk blouse, then dropped it to the side. She still held his gaze because that was all heat and demand, and better, somehow, than accepting the fact that she was standing before Balthazar Skalas wearing nothing but her bra and some panties.

She realized he'd gone still. As if he'd

turned to stone, though there was absolutely no doubt that he was a real, live man. Even if made of flesh, she suspected he would scald her if she leaned across the desk and touched him.

Why did she want to do it anyway?

Kendra didn't wait for him to egg her on further. She reached around and unhooked her bra, then shrugged it off.

He made a sound then, perhaps nothing more than a breath, but it was like fireworks going off inside of her—bright and hot and uncontrollable.

She fought it, but her own breath came faster, then.

It was as if there was an electrical charge between them, too intense. Almost painful.

But she wasn't done. She couldn't dwell on what was happening inside of her, because she still felt a kind of drumming in her chest, threatening her ribs, that made her feel as if she *needed* to show him exactly how wrong he was about her.

So Kendra finished the job, stripping off

her panties and dropping them on top of the pile of her clothes.

Leaving her…standing there. Stark naked.

And though her cheeks were hot and she felt certain that the flush extended all over the rest of her body, though she was *aware* that she had so many competing emotions it actually hurt, she couldn't access the things she was feeling. Not quite.

Because his gaze was all over her.

And then, to her horror—*no, no*, a voice in her chided, *that's not* horror *and you know it*—Balthazar moved out from behind the desk.

He hadn't said he would touch her, and she assured herself that if he did, if he dared, she would—

But that was a lie. It wasn't even a fully formed thought and it was a lie.

Because the thought of Balthazar touching her made her shiver. That low heat bloomed.

And once again, she was as slippery and hot, as if he'd just finished stroking his way deep into her core.

Maybe she wanted him to.

But all he did was come to stand before her, that cruel face of his unreadable.

If it weren't for that blazing heat in his dark gaze, she might have crumpled into the pile of her discarded clothes.

He let her stand there as he regarded her for what felt to Kendra like a lifetime. Three lifetimes.

Then he walked in a circle around her.

As if she was a horse.

"Do you need to inspect my teeth?" she asked. Acidly.

"Not yet."

She had to bite her tongue again, particularly as he took his sweet time. She could *feel* him and his dark perusal. His gaze was like a touch, running all over her, tracing over her body and making her pulse get faster and faster by the second.

When he finally made his way around the front again, it was almost worse. Her breasts felt heavy once more, the way she remembered they had in that gazebo years ago. Beneath his commanding gaze, her nipples puckered and shamed her. Because she could tell herself that it was the chill from his air-conditioning units, but she knew better. And so, she could see, did he.

He let his gaze drop, coming to rest between her thighs. And Kendra was absurdly grateful that he couldn't see what was happening there. He couldn't see how much she truly wanted him.

Even though something in her whispered that he could.

"How extraordinary," Balthazar murmured after a while. "I was sure that color had to be fake."

She had no idea what he meant. But then, when he lifted his gaze to hers again, she got it.

And hated the fact that her cheeks burst into a brighter flame. She could feel it roll all the way over her body, like a flash flood of heat, so that she likely matched the hair on her head and between her legs that he'd apparently found so hard to believe was real. She felt *red* and *obvious,* and had to grit her teeth to keep from diving for cover.

"There are so many things I find surprising

about you, *kopéla,*" Balthazar continued on, as if this was a deeply boring dinner party and he was sharing his views on something distressingly civil and dry. As if she wasn't *naked* before him. Why did that make it even harder to pull in a full breath? "This shocking show of obedience, for example. I would have said a girl of your station would find it impossible."

She made herself breathe, somehow. "I told you I was here to make amends, if possible."

"Naked amends." As if she might have missed that. He considered her for a moment, that face of his stern. "What a good daughter you are, Kendra. Far more of a sister than your brother deserves, don't you think?"

She didn't answer that.

"How far does this obedience extend, I wonder?" He stood before her, the devil in a dark suit that fit him much too well, fully aware of his power. Exultant in it, even. "If I asked you to drop to your knees and take me in your mouth, would you? If I bent you over this desk and took my release without bothering to see to your pleasure, would you allow it? There are so many options available to us, are there not? So many ways to audition, after all."

And somehow, it was only then that it occurred to Kendra to take stock of the precariousness of her position.

It was only then that she really thought about what she was doing here.

Because her head was filled with new images now. Balthazar doing exactly what he'd just told her he might. She could see it too clearly—too vividly—and she couldn't decide if it seemed like peril or passion. To sink to her knees, tilt her head back, and taste the most male part of him. Or to be tossed across the vast expanse of his desk as if she'd been put on this earth with no other thought but to please him, when and how he wished...

She couldn't decide if those things terrified her. Or if they didn't.

"Look at you," he mused, his voice a dark, rough abrasion. She felt her skin prickle, breaking out into goose bumps. "So eager to please."

She was breathing too hard, after failing to

breathe at all for a while. She couldn't seem to speak.

And then he made it worse by reaching out and fitting his hand to her cheek.

It was not a soft, caring sort of gesture.

He might as well have slid it straight between her legs. Again.

Kendra shook so hard she thought her bones might have flown apart. She had to check a moan, but it still made her teeth rattle.

Balthazar laughed, dark and terrible. "You're not a martyr at all, are you, Kendra?" he asked quietly. Cruelly. "You're just a little whore."

It took her too long to register those words. Even longer to understand them.

And when she did, when that blow landed the way it was clearly meant to, she actually staggered back.

But by then, he had already walked out and left her there.

Naked, in his office, alone and sick with shame.

It was as if all the blood that had been pumping inside of her drained away, and suddenly she was freezing cold. Her teeth began to chatter. Her hands felt thick and unwieldy, but she did the best she could to hurriedly climb back into the clothes she'd discarded.

What was she thinking? How had she let this happen?

How had she actually *wanted*—

But none of that mattered, she told herself sternly, shutting it down. This was no time to spiral. There would be all the time in the world for that.

What mattered now was that he hadn't agreed to anything.

He could have left his office to call the authorities *right now*, and all of this would have been for nothing.

Kendra didn't think she could survive it.

When she was finally dressed again, she took an extra moment with her reflection in the mirror on the far wall. Because her skin might have been several shades too red for comfort, but she thought she really might die if she marched back out into all that corporate luxury…disheveled. So clearly a fool.

Her breasts were still too sensitive. She was horrifyingly damp between her legs. But none of that mattered, not yet. Kendra imagined she'd have the rest of her life to regret, deeply, what had happened here. But right now she needed to figure out how not to disappoint her father.

She headed toward the door, her mind racing. She should have expected that Balthazar would want to humiliate her. Clearly he wanted to humiliate the entire Connolly family—which, if she was honest, she couldn't really blame him for. Two million dollars wasn't exactly pocket change.

Okay, maybe it was for Balthazar Skalas.

Kendra couldn't blame him for wanting to punish someone who'd stolen from him, so she focused on the real culprit in all this. Her brother. If she allowed herself, she would get so furious with Tommy that it might take her to her knees—

And she really didn't want to think about being on her knees. Not after Balthazar had introduced an entirely new way of thinking about kneeling to her today.

She strode out, still trying to come up with a new game plan, and then stopped dead.

Because Balthazar was there, leaning against the long, white wall that served as his gallery, waiting. And the way his gaze found hers, she understood that this interaction had gone exactly as he'd intended it to.

That helped. It reminded her why she was here—what was at stake.

And how little it had to do with those maddening sensations he stirred up in her.

This is your chance to prove you're valuable, she reminded herself sternly. *Don't waste it.*

"I'm disappointed," she said briskly as she walked toward him, ordering her knees not to buckle beneath her. Because there could be no *kneeling,* God help her. "I expected better of you than cheap, juvenile name-calling."

"Did you? I can't think why."

"Not to mention, I would have thought that a man who trafficked in mistresses would prefer an experienced practitioner. Or are you under the impression that a woman who accepts a mercenary position as your mistress somehow… isn't?"

"Don't be silly," Balthazar said, a kind of

dark humor in his voice. "A good mistress always pretends that she would never, ever succumb to anyone else."

"Surely, once again, what you mean is an accomplished proficient. Isn't the expectation that she'll always make the client feel as if, were it only up to her, she'd be doing it for free?"

He let out a bark of laughter. Real laughter, Kendra thought, when she nearly missed a step. Her heart didn't know how to process it.

All kinds of parts of her didn't know how to process it.

She stood there a few feet away from him, stricken, too aware of the way that laughter licked its way through her. And equally aware that despite her best attempts here—despite actually removing her clothing and standing there naked before this man—she had failed.

He was laughing at her. He had already rejected her.

What else did she have to offer him?

"You must go back to your father and your brother and tell them about these offers you have made me," Balthazar said, when his laughter finally stopped. He straightened from the wall, and she was struck anew by the *physicality* of this man. Unlike the rest of her father's associates that she'd met over the years, there wasn't the faintest hint of dissipation stamped on his skin. No paunch, no alcoholic redness about his cheeks. Just that glare of his, like smoke and condemnation—and all else a pageant of lean muscle and tightly leashed power. "How proud the two of them will be, I am certain, that you are prepared to go to these lengths for them. The obvious next question is, how often have you done exactly this on their command?"

"That's more of a philosophical question, really," she made herself say, trying to sound witty and urbane. Or something other than shattered. "Are fallen women born or made, do you think?"

It was only as his expression changed, shifting to something far more heated and intent, that she realized that she'd been backing up. That he was advancing on her. And she really ought to have stood there, stood her ground—

But she didn't have it in her. She was still

trembling, from the inside out, and he was bearing down on her.

She could either kneel or back away, and she didn't dare kneel.

Kendra was terrified that she might not want to do anything else once she did.

"The philosophy of fallen women," Balthazar said in a musing sort of voice, though there was nothing *musing* in the way he looked at her, then. "I confess I have never given it any thought."

"Of course not. Why think of such things when all that is necessary is using and discarding them on a whim?"

She threw the words at him as if she thought they might hurt him. As if she thought anything might hurt him.

His mouth moved into something even more cruel. Her breath caught. Then Kendra had the confusing sensation of moving through something—only belatedly realizing that he'd backed her straight through the door of his office again.

"Shall we test your theory?" he asked, his voice a growl.

She was something like bewitched. She could only watch as he reached out a hand again, sliding it along her jaw, his fingers over her lips, then hooking the nape of her neck as he had long ago.

Her breath was a wild, flickering flame between them—

Then Balthazar's mouth was on hers, obliterating everything else but need.

CHAPTER FOUR

HE SHOULD HAVE let her go.

That had been Balthazar's plan. Humiliate her, then dismiss her.

A neat revenge for how she'd left him in that gazebo three years ago. Also a slap at her father and brother, who kept aiming their tawdry secret weapon at him. He'd been looking forward to aiming it right back in their direction, without giving them even a shred of what they'd wanted from him in return.

Only a small taste of what he had in store for Thomas Connolly and his spawn.

He had been congratulating himself on a job well done while he waited for her to slink out, her proverbial tail between her legs.

But she'd come out of his office tucked neatly back into the sleek skirt and blouse she'd worn. There hadn't been the faintest hint of any slinking. It was as if nothing happened in there. There was only some turbulence in her gaze.

And that husky note in her voice.

Balthazar honestly didn't know what had come over him. Maybe it was when she hadn't wilted away into nothing when he'd used the word *whore*.

When she'd debated the point instead.

He had been unable to control himself. Or more precisely, perfectly able to control himself, a skill that had been beaten into him by his merciless father—but wholly uninterested in doing so.

And now his mouth was on hers, at last.

At last.

The half-formed notion he might have had that he'd mistaken things three years ago, along with any story he might have been tempted to tell himself about the ways he'd convinced himself it had been more than it was, disappeared as if they'd never been.

Because the taste of Kendra was far better than any memory.

It was the richness of her mouth, the way

her lips met his. It was the slickness. The heat. It was better than anything he could have imagined. *She* was better.

Worth the wait, a voice inside whispered.

He tried to shove it aside, but something in him...snapped.

As if he truly had been waiting for her all this time, instead of merely interested that an opportunity to pay her back had arisen.

As if this was what he'd wanted all along. This. Her.

He reached out blindly with his free hand and slammed his office door shut. That was the last thought he planned to give to the outside world. He moved her across his floor, every cell in his body focused on the same thing.

More.

Kendra had as much as told him she was precisely who and what he'd thought she was all along. She'd offered herself to him. Attempted to barter the terms of selling herself to her family's enemy. Despite what he'd imagined in those first moments in that long-ago gazebo, she was no innocent.

He told himself that was a gift.

Because it turned out that Balthazar was in no way above taking what she'd made it clear was his to take.

Surely he'd initially meant to aim for the sofa that sat across the room, but it was suddenly too far. He made it to his desk and laid her down across the vast granite surface, making her its only adornment.

Like a sacrificial lamb, something in him thought, though that was a reach. This was no sacrifice.

This was a reckoning.

Balthazar couldn't seem to get enough of her mouth. He braced himself over her, his palm near her head, and lost himself for far too long in the simple act of kissing her.

Again and again.

But there was nothing simple about it.

It was carnal. It was a rush. The taste of her coursed through him, storming through his veins and pooling in his sex.

More than worth the wait, that voice in him said, more definitively this time.

Like a kick to the side of his head. Balthazar tore his mouth away from hers, outraged that he felt as close to shaky in the presence of a woman as he'd ever become.

Shaky, of all things. When his father had made him pay hefty prices for weakness. Until now, Balthazar had been certain he'd stamped any hint of his out.

And it was only when he set his mouth to Kendra's neck, finding that raucous pulse again, that it finally dawned on him that he hadn't kissed her three years ago. No wonder a simple taste of her had set his head to ringing.

He wanted to strip her naked again, but he wasn't certain he could handle it.

That truth was humbling.

He, Balthazar Skalas, who had proven himself again and again in the course of his lifetime whether he wished to or not. Against his father's heavy hand, his mother's defection. Against fair-weather friends and false intimates. The trials of handling both the Skalas's wealth and business concerns with all the questionable, obsequious grifters both attracted.

He had always assumed that his ruthlessness was bone-deep.

But this mercenary little liar, an emissary from a man he despised, who wanted her to trade her body for her thieving waste of a brother—

Why on earth should it be this girl who got to him like this?

He could see her body still, as if she hadn't put her clothes back on. He could see how she'd stood before him, not unaffected by her nudity, but not cringing or cowering, either.

He thought of his beloved Greece and all the great statues of goddesses, breasts bared, bodies more weapons of awe than shame.

And he thought that for the rest of his life when he looked at such pieces of art he would see Kendra instead. Small yet plump breasts with rosy crests. The tempting slope of her belly. The auburn tangle of curls at the apex of her thighs.

Somehow, with the taste of her in his mouth, he thought that if he stripped her again it might kill him.

That was absurd, of course.

But even so, he reached down and began to tug her skirt up instead of removing it. She made a wordless sort of noise, then lifted her hips, helping him clear the fabric from around her hips.

He could smell her arousal.

It made him think of gardens before a summer storm, heavy with scent. Flowers and a raw bloom.

It almost made him lose himself completely.

Balthazar didn't understand what was happening inside of him.

She was spread out before him, his entirely for the taking if the blissed-out look on her face was any clue, and he should have felt cynical and triumphant at once.

He'd had any number of beautiful women below him before, but this was different. This was Kendra Connolly. And much as he might like to imagine otherwise, he had been imagining something like this for very long time indeed.

There was a part of him that had been thrilled to discover that her vile brother had been foolish enough to get himself into such trouble.

Had he hoped that this would happen? He had expected her to offer, but had he hoped all along that he would accept that offer—even though he'd assured himself that he was only taking this meeting for the chance to humiliate a Connolly?

He had to face the fact that this was exactly what he'd wanted.

Balthazar felt something like drunk, when he never allowed himself such indulgences.

But her legs were free of the constriction of her skirt then, so he stepped between them, pulling her bottom to the edge of the granite desk.

Her arms seem to move of their own accord, rising over her head. She arched back with a kind of inbred grace that poured through him, a new kind of storm. Looking at her made his chest feel tight.

But he shoved all of that aside and concentrated on the part of him that ached for her the most.

Balthazar reached down to unzip himself,

then pull his own throbbing length free. Finally.

He heard an indrawn breath and when he looked up again, Kendra's eyes seemed even wider and brighter, and she was biting down on her bottom lip.

And he felt something sharp move in him then, like fragments of broken glass, embedding themselves in his flesh.

She was the very picture of innocence on the verge of surrender, wasn't she? Balthazar could admit, deep inside himself where he would never discuss it with another living soul or admit it out loud, that there was no small part of him that wished the picture she presented was real.

That had been the issue three years ago. It was worse now.

He reached between her legs and pulled her panties to one side. Then, giving in to the brute in him, he tore them off her and tossed them aside. He could see goose bumps rise on the smooth flesh of her inner thighs and wasn't surprised when she covered her face with her arms, because they both knew the truth, didn't they?

She wanted him. This was the game. And better she should hide now that he was winning it.

If he had been more in control of himself, he wouldn't have allowed it. He'd have pinned her hands above her head, bent close, and studied her face as he thrust deep into the very center of her molten heat.

He'd have enjoyed every moment of this victory.

But this was far wilder than he'd anticipated. Whatever it was that beat in him, it made him feel savage. Something like mad with it.

She was too hot, too wet.

He felt himself growl, like the beast only she brought out in him, and then he simply slammed himself home.

She arched up against him and he gripped her hips, because she felt so good. She was impossibly tight and hot around him, and for a heady beat or two of his heart he thought he might finish there and then.

Surely not.

Balthazar braced himself against the desk, fighting for control. And as he did, he became aware that she was breathing rapidly. Her chest was moving, and there was a deep red flush all over her neck.

"Show me your face," he ordered her.

He felt her clench down hard, internally, and swore as that tight grip nearly threw him over the edge. She moved her hips almost tentatively and held her arms in place, tighter, for a few more moments before she let her arms fall.

Her face looked even more flushed than her neck, her eyes so bright it made him freeze. Almost as if she was on the verge of tears— but that made no sense.

"I don't understand why we're stopping," she threw at him. Reminding him that this was a fight, and no matter if there was a strange note in her voice as she spoke. He could see the echo of it reflected in her too-bright gaze, burning like the sweet, hot center of an open fire. "This is what you wanted, surely. Do it."

A kind of alarm rang in him at that, but she made a greedy sort of sound and then locked her ankles in the small of his back.

And then, her eyes fastened fiercely to his, she began to move her hips.

It was crude and inelegant and, oddly, the most erotic thing he could ever recall happening to him.

There was something about the determination on her flushed face. The way she moved, taking all of him, then retreating, over and over, her teeth almost bared as if she was determined to get this right.

He'd expected practiced moves, soft laughter.

What he got instead was…this fierce attack of pleasure that should have put him off.

Balthazar thought it might be the hottest thing he'd ever seen.

And it felt like magic.

He slid his hands beneath her and lifted her up, gripping the soft curves of her bottom and holding her before him so he could take control.

He started slow, matching her deliberateness. Her intensity.

Stroke after stroke, deep and hard, so there could be no mistake about who he was. Who she was. What was happening here.

And something extraordinary happened as he kept going, communicating the truth of things the only way he could. That sheen of ferocity seemed to mellow, as if the heat between them was doing the same work in her as it was in him. The sharpness in her gaze became something else, something molten.

He kept on, maintaining a deliberate rhythm even as he watched a different kind of heat wash over her.

And when she stiffened again, her head fell back in that same beautiful surrender he recalled years ago.

Once again, Kendra cried out heedlessly as she shattered all around him.

He wanted more. He wanted everything. He *wanted*.

Balthazar dropped down and set his mouth against her neck. His hips pounded into her, faster and faster. He reached between them and found the proud center of her need, then worked it with his fingers as he finally, greedily, cast off what few chains of control remained.

And let himself go wild.

This time, when she screamed she bucked against him, hurtling straight off that edge and taking him with her.

But the noise he made felt torn from deep inside him as he followed her over.

Ruined, that voice in him whispered.

And Balthazar could do nothing about it. He was…broken into pieces, sprawled over her without breath.

For a long while there was only the way their hearts thundered, almost as if to the same beat.

He wanted to gather her to him. He wanted to do things that made no sense, like press kisses against the line of her jaw. When it finally penetrated that he felt the urge to do these mad things, it was like dousing himself in a cold plunge.

Balthazar pulled out, though it caused him

something almost like pain to leave behind that silken grip.

He told himself to turn away abruptly, but he didn't. He took his time, fully aware that it was likely to be burned into him forever, the sight of her like this. Sprawled out on his desk, her skirt rucked up to her waist, thoroughly debauched and thoroughly his.

You're a fool, he growled at himself. *That was revenge and nothing more.*

But that felt very much like a lie, when he had long considered himself allergic to dishonesty in any form.

When he finished putting himself to rights, he focused on her and found her doing the same. Her eyes were downcast as she slid from the desk. And though she tugged her skirt back into place competently enough, her hair told a different story.

Balthazar did not advise her to smooth it down. A clear indication that no matter how smooth an exterior she tried to present, the reality remained.

He liked that more than he should have.

"Shall we consider that a down payment?"

she asked, her voice so crisp and cold that it took him a moment to realize she hadn't actually hauled off and slapped him.

And he chose not to question why it felt like a betrayal. When he knew it shouldn't. When he knew who she was.

Who she always had been. Why did he insist on wishing it could be otherwise?

"Don't be ridiculous, Kendra," he replied in kind. "That was merely finishing what we started three years ago."

He watched the column of her throat move. He was suddenly, deeply furious that she wouldn't raise her head and look at him directly. "Surely it can be both."

Balthazar made himself laugh and took some pride in how she stiffened at the sound.

"I wouldn't pay two dollars for something I could get so easily, *kopéla*. Much less two million."

Her gaze snapped to his then, bright and hot.

And worse, a kind of knowledge flickering there in the depths that made everything in him tighten. Sending him into a spiral of something perilously close to shame.

Especially when she didn't crumple before him.

She held herself almost regally. "Shall I tell my brother to expect to see you in court?"

"You can tell your brother to go to hell," he growled at her, because he didn't care for the sensation still curling around and around inside of him. He didn't acknowledge shame. But he could still feel her, clenched tight around him. And the taste of her was in his mouth. And all of it was part of the same game. He would never forgive it. "You can go right along with him, for all I care."

He saw her gaze grow brighter and he thought once again that she might sob. He didn't know what he would do if she did—

But instead, she only nodded, once.

"Understood," she said icily.

Then Balthazar watched as Kendra Connolly marched over to his door, threw it open, and left as if she'd never been here.

As if she'd never screamed his name while he was buried deep inside her. Twice.

Leaving behind nothing but a torn bit of lace that had once been her panties.

Balthazar stood there a long, long while. His phone rang. His mobile buzzed. He heard one of his secretaries come to the door and say his name, then retreat when he failed to respond.

Outside the walls of windows, New York was a mess of color and noise.

Like her.

While inside, Balthazar was nothing but cold.

So cold that it took him much, much longer than it should have to realize that for the first time in his life, he had not only failed to use protection with a woman—and not just any woman, the daughter of the man who Balthazar had long ago vowed to destroy if it took him his whole life—it had not so much as crossed his mind.

CHAPTER FIVE

THREE MONTHS LATER, Kendra had succeeded in convincing herself that what had happened at Skalas Tower was some kind of bad dream.

Well. She called it a bad dream in the light of day. What a nightmare! What a horror!

But the more unpalatable truth was that sometimes she woke in the night, convinced that she could feel all that thick, hot masculinity moving inside her again. Sure that if she blinked away the sleep from her eyes she would see his face, so stern and sensual at once, right there above her as he blocked out the world…

The way she felt in the dark had nothing to do with horror. She was wise enough to keep that to herself.

Because she had better things to think about than one evening of pure insanity three months ago. Such as finding herself a new life because, like it or not, she'd left the old one in tatters on the floor of Balthazar's office that night, and there was no pretending otherwise.

Her father and brother had not been impressed when Kendra had returned that night without any good news to report. She had been similarly unimpressed to find them both waiting up for her, since the drive back out from New York City had in no way allowed her to settle down after...him.

"Well?" Tommy had demanded.

Angrily, as if waiting for his baby sister to return from this vile errand was beneath him.

When it was *for* him.

He had been swilling his gin and looking at her in disgust, neither of which was new. But after her intense, provoking experience earlier, something inside of her had... Not *snapped*, exactly. But she'd stripped naked in front of Balthazar Skalas. She'd argued for leniency and she'd bartered herself, all for the brother who was making no secret of how little he cared for her.

Why are you trying to help this person? an unfamiliar voice asked from deep down inside her. *When he would quite clearly never, ever so much as consider doing the same for you?*

Kendra had never thought about it quite like that before. Once she had, she couldn't think of anything else. Why was she trying to prove herself to him? Or her father?

Why do you feel you have anything to prove?

She couldn't answer that question, either.

It was as if letting Balthazar inside her body had changed her, profoundly.

Not simply the act itself, which she couldn't quite let herself think about at that point— too overwhelming and raw, painful and then transcendent, all mixed in together—but the *fact* of it.

She didn't feel like the same naive creature who had set off in her sensible shoes, so determined to fight off a dragon and save her family. She wasn't the same. The dragon had eaten her alive and there was no pretending otherwise.

That had been the first evidence of how

different she was after her encounter with Balthazar. The fact that she could see her selfish, petulant brother for who he was and feel no matching surge of need to prove herself any further.

"What exactly did you think would happen?" she'd asked as she stood in the door of her father's study. And after matching wits with Balthazar Skalas, she'd rather thought her brother unequal to the task. "Did you really think that a man like that could be tempted into forgetting what you did to him?"

"I hope you're not saying that you struck out, girl," her father had grumbled from his favorite armchair. "That's not what you're saying, is it?"

Even then, Kendra had wanted badly to tell herself that he'd wanted her to succeed because he believed in her. And not because he'd wanted her to sort out Tommy's mess.

But she'd lost her ability to fool herself that night.

"I tried my best," she had said, because what else was there to say? Even if she'd told them what she'd done, they wouldn't understand. They hadn't been there. They wouldn't get the weight of her surrender. That exquisite tension that had flared between her and Balthazar that she'd still been able to feel tight around her, like his hands around her throat. Or his palm between her legs. She'd shrugged instead. "I tried and I failed. I don't know what he's going to do now."

"You frigid bitch," Tommy had snarled at her. And even though their father had made a tutting sort of noise, Tommy hadn't retracted it. He hadn't backed down. Instead, he'd taken the tumbler he was holding and threw it so that it exploded against the stone of the fireplace. "I told you not to go dressed like that. Of course you failed. Just *look* at you! You look like a dowdy, frumpy, boring secretary. Who would want that?"

She'd stared back at her brother, seeing his sulky expression and remembering Balthazar's beautiful, brutal masculinity. His grace and ferocity. Tommy had not done well by comparison.

"I can only wonder why you were pinning all your hopes on me if I'm so deficient," she'd said calmly. Almost coldly. "There's nothing more that I can do. And if I'm honest, I think I've already done too much—particularly if this is the thanks I get."

Kendra had turned and marched from the room, paying no attention when she heard her brother's voice raised in fury behind her. She had not glanced at her father again. She'd had the revolutionary thought, after everything, that what happened next to the pair of them had nothing to do with her.

Instead, she'd run up the stairs to her childhood bedroom, locked the door behind her, and then crumpled down on the other side of it. She'd hugged her knees to her chest, held herself tight, and tried to figure out what to do with herself now everything had changed.

Now that she had changed.

Now that she knew the things she knew. Now that she'd finally faced the truth.

Kendra had wanted to dissolve into sobs, but hadn't. She'd breathed a little too heavily for a while, ragged and overwhelmed, and had eventually found her way into the shower. There she'd done her best to use up all the hot water on the eastern seaboard as she'd done her best to scrub off the evening she'd had.

She'd failed at that, too.

It was only later, when she'd tucked herself up in her childish canopy bed as if that could make her the girl she'd been again, that she'd finally allowed herself to go through the whole thing, step by step.

He'd braced himself above her, so fierce, almost furious.

And he'd called her a whore, so Kendra had been determined that he never suspect that she was anything but. She'd told herself that she was a modern woman, after all. She'd ridden horses her whole life. Surely, if she didn't tell him, he would never know that she'd never let anyone close to her before. That she'd been too busy trying to be perfect in one way or another, and had never seen how a boyfriend fit into that.

It won't hurt, she'd told herself. *If it hurt as much as people claimed it did, no one would do it again.*

Then Balthazar had slammed his way inside her, and it was as if he'd plugged her into an electrical outlet, the most fragile part of her first.

Her first reaction had been shock.

Her body had reacted without her permission, arching up in a way that could as easily have been surrender as a scream. She hadn't known herself.

She'd hidden her face, bitten down on her own arm, and it was only when her teeth dug into her own flesh that she'd begun to sort through the storm of it all.

Pain wasn't the right word. She'd felt *everything*, that was the trouble. The shock of his intrusion. The shape of him, lodged deep inside of her. Big, hot, long. There was *a person inside her*, and that notion made her want to cry even as it sent spirals of a different sensation dancing through her.

He'd told her to drop her arms, she'd obeyed, and again she'd been swept up in the certainty that if she let him see that this was her first time, if she let him know that this was anything but what she wanted it to be, she would die.

Die.

So instead, she'd dared him to do it faster. Harder. Deeper.

But when he did, everything had changed again.

And by the time they were finished, Kendra had learned a great many things about herself.

In the three months since that night, she'd had a lot of time to think about those things.

That she was not at all who she'd always thought she was if she could be so easily taken. Not just taken, but possessed, fully. A man who hated her could do those things to her body, and more astonishingly, her body could respond to him with pure jubilation.

No matter what *she* might have thought about the situation.

If that was true, and Kendra knew it was, then she didn't know herself at all. And if she didn't know herself at all, if she even now found herself something like hungry, constantly going over that night in Balthazar's office in her head—

She'd concluded mere days after that fateful night that she needed to change her life entirely.

And so she had.

Her Great-Aunt Rosemary, the despair of Kendra's haughty Grandmother Patricia, had taken herself off to the French countryside rather than settle down into marriage the way her parents would have preferred. She had never bothered to return to the family, but she'd left Kendra her cottage when she'd died the previous year.

On the off chance you are not like your mother or hers, Great-Aunt Rosemary's will had read, *I offer you a place to land.*

Kendra had always meant to make it over to inspect her inheritance...someday.

Someday had turned out to be a lot sooner than she'd imagined.

"Don't be ridiculous," her father had thundered at her when she'd announced her plans to remove herself to the French countryside. At once. "What on earth do you plan to do in *France*, of all places?"

"Whatever I like," she'd replied. "Would

you like me to stay? That will only happen if you give me a job in the company."

"Kendra. Sweetheart." The unusual endearment had shocked them both, and her father had looked away. "I don't see the company as a part of your future."

She'd braced herself for the pain of that to swipe at her, but there had been nothing. As if she'd finally moved past it. "Then what does it matter where I choose to live?"

And that was how she'd found her way to her great-aunt's lovely little cottage, suspended between the mountains and the sea. Nestled amid rolling vineyards on country roads, the cottage itself was a bookish girl's dream. A few bright, happy rooms filled with books and art, paths through the fields to walk on, and more than a few trees with abundant shade if she wanted a break from the glorious Côte d'Azur sunshine.

She went down into Nice to do her shopping, and it was easy enough to drive down into Italy, or take the long train ride to Paris. She told herself it was the best few months of her life.

She wanted it to be. Desperately.

And if sometimes Kendra felt so melancholy that she almost got sick with it, she dismissed it as growing pains. She was lucky enough to be in the position to take a time-out to figure out what her life ought to be. Accordingly, she tried to imagine what her life would look like now if she took the family company off the table. If she stopped pushing so hard.

Maybe it was a good thing that she wasn't working with her father and brother now that she'd lost a huge amount of her respect for them. But Kendra had always wanted to work. She had no interest in the kind of highly charged, gossip-soaked idleness her mother preferred—and no aptitude for it, if she was honest.

All the sorts of play jobs other women in her position had, she dismissed. Virtuous charities with flashy balls, prized internships only those with trust funds could afford to take, silly publicity positions that were usually about getting on the guest lists to highly photographed parties. None of that appealed to her. Kendra tried to encourage herself to think outside the box. She'd been so focused on getting into her father's good graces that she'd never spent any time imagining what would happen if that…stopped mattering to her.

Because it didn't. The further away she got from that night with Balthazar, the more angry she found herself.

Not at Tommy, who had never made a secret of who he was or pretended to be anything else. Not Balthazar, who was wholly and completely himself, always.

But at her father.

Her father, who had preferred that his daughter give herself to a man he considered an enemy than deal with Tommy's behavior himself. Tommy had put the company, the family, and his own sister into peril—but that hadn't inspired her father to handle him, once and for all. And at no time had Thomas Connolly thought, *Maybe it would be smart to try out the one child who* hasn't *caused me problems.*

Kendra was humiliated she hadn't seen all of this before. It wasn't as if anyone had hidden it. She'd simply seen what she'd wanted to see. She'd believed that if she worked hard enough, there was a way for her to take her rightful place at her father's side. All she had to do was prove it.

Now she thought that if given the chance, she'd burn the whole Connolly family down. Great-Aunt Rosemary had clearly had the right idea.

A darling little cottage tucked away in the south of France was the perfect opportunity for Kendra to uncover her heretofore unknown artistic leanings, she'd figured. She kept a journal. She tried a bit of creative writing. She took a painting class. A pottery class. She tried to learn how to play piano.

But by the end of her second month in France, neck deep in all things Provençal, it was clear that Kendra had no aptitude whatsoever for anything creative.

Not even the faintest shred of it.

And that was how she'd found herself at one of the local wineries nestled away in a glorious, sweeping vineyard down the road from her cottage. The owners thought it would be helpful to have an American on hand for the summer to help with tourists, and Kendra quickly found that her real aptitude was in customer service, of all things.

Because she was fantastic at it. And more, enjoyed it.

It was a beautiful summer afternoon. The breeze was scented with lavender and the hint of earth. Groups of tasters and merrymakers had come to enjoy the vineyard and its offerings, some coming up from the crowded beaches along this magical stretch of coastline, some engaged in winery tours, and some on self-guided explorations of the area. They sat in merry little clusters at the tiled tables out beneath bright blue umbrellas and graceful trellises wrapped in jasmine and wisteria vines.

Kendra moved from table to table, making sure everyone had the food they'd ordered from the small kitchen or the sommelier's attention. She got to use the French she'd taken in boarding school and college or her English, depending on the group. And maybe there was something wrong with her, she thought when she ducked back inside to see if the kitchen was ready with the charcuterie platters one of her groups had ordered. There had to be, because most people surely didn't find it easier to know themselves while they were interacting with strangers. Or not know herself, perhaps. But feel at ease with herself all the same.

Because to all the customers sitting at these tables, she was nothing but an American girl on a lark. Enjoying herself abroad, perfectly carefree.

And the more they treated her that way, the more she believed it was the truth.

No Connolly family power struggles. No demands she marry a member of her mother's yacht club, the red-shorts-wearing hedge fund brigade. No contending with Tommy and his latest fiasco.

Carefree felt *good*.

Kendra had her back to the door when it opened again. She sang out a greeting in French as she picked up the two heavy plates of charcuterie that the chef arranged in glorious piles of the finest meats and cheeses, all arranged on their own private stones.

"Please take a menu and find a seat outside," she said over her shoulder. "I'll be with you in a moment."

She turned as she spoke, her happy carefree smile on her face.

But it was not a new group of tourists.

It was Balthazar.

He did not speak. But then, he didn't have to speak when all he did was reach up and remove the mirrored sunglasses from his face, letting that blazing dark gaze slam straight into her.

He was Balthazar Skalas.

That harsh look on his face was as good as another man's shout.

Kendra would never know how she managed to keep holding those heavy platters aloft. Possibly it was that she was frozen solid. Turned to stone.

Incapable of anything but staring at the apparition before her.

One ice age passed. Then another.

"Excuse me," she said in totally unnecessary French. "I must deliver these."

She hardly knew what she was doing, only that it was critical she do it. She set off across the floor, then ducked out the door to the patio while he stood there beside it like a smoldering ember.

Outside, she smiled and laughed on cue. She set down the platter and then spent a long, long time telling the group at the table the involved history of every cheese, cured meat, and olive. Only when she'd exhausted that topic did she turn back and head inside.

Slowly, having half convinced herself that Balthazar was a figment of her imagination.

But no.

He was still there, in the exact same place where she'd left him. The devil himself, so incongruous in a French winery's tasting kitchen that she almost laughed at the absurdity.

Almost. Because there was very little about Balthazar in his considerably mouthwatering flesh that made her feel like laughing.

Another eon or two dragged by as she

stared at him. As he returned the favor with the full force of his stern regard.

It took everything Kendra had to fight off all the images that threatened to flood her then. The memories of what had happened between them.

"You must connect these dots for me," Balthazar said. Eventually. His voice was as she remembered it. Dark. Stirring. Dangerous. "Tell me how a Connecticut heiress finds herself a waitress half a world away."

"As it happens, I have an innate talent for customer service," she replied, using her brightest, happiest tone, as if he was really interested in her answer. "That's not something I knew before I came to France."

"How can it surprise you?" His voice only got more lethal. More than that, it was a whole storm inside her, so that not only was she forced to remember every single thing that had happened that night in Manhattan, she could *feel* it. Her body was reliving it, one sensation after the next. "Look what you were willing to do for your brother. How could you doubt that it was a...talent, as you say?"

"I'm delighted you haven't changed a bit." She forced her usual happy smile. "Have you come for a tasting? I handle the food, but if you take a seat on the terrace, the sommelier will be with you shortly and can lead you on the journey of your choice through our wines. Today we're featuring—"

"If I wished to sample wine, Kendra, I would not come here. I have my own vine-yards."

She rolled her eyes. "As one does."

His face tightened. "I still do not under-stand. Are you hiding?" If possible, his gaze darkened. "Do you have some reason to hide?"

"This is the south of France," Kendra said, frowning at him. "People do not *hide* here. They spend their entire lives concocting rea-sons to come visit. Then come back. Then find a picturesque cottage surrounded by sunflowers and lavender to grow old in. It's paradise, Balthazar. Who wouldn't want to live in paradise?"

"You surprise me. I would have expected you to stay tethered to the family apron strings, running errands for your father and brother. That is your role, is it not?"

She pulled in a breath, surprised at how much that hurt. When really, Kendra had been expecting something like that the moment she'd seen him.

"Don't beat around the bush," she said softly. "If you want to call me names, call me names."

One of his dark brows rose. "Did I not do so?"

"I'm afraid I've stepped away from my former profession." She managed to use her usual bright and shiny voice, and took some pride in the fact she could when he'd left her bleeding. If she didn't show it, that was almost as good as not bleeding at all. "If that's why you've come, you're going to be deeply disappointed."

Balthazar pushed away from the wall, then prowled around the small shop with its souvenirs and keepsakes along one wall, the refrigerated case filled with takeaway options, and the menu stand for table service.

Somehow, Kendra had never realized how small the place was before. How…close.

But then, Balthazar took all the air from the room.

"If you have business with my family, you know how to find them," she said after a moment, though her pulse was drumming loudly in her ears. "I have nothing to do with this."

"Perhaps."

His back was to her then. His gaze was directed out the windows, down over the gentle slope of the vineyard before them. The view she'd loved, until now. Would she ever be able to look at it again without seeing him?

"Tell me this, if you please," he was saying, low and commanding. "It has been some time since I saw you in New York."

"Since you saw me," she echoed, and even laughed. "How sanitized that sounds."

Balthazar turned to her. She thought the way his gaze cut through her was stark. Brooding, even. But he didn't speak.

"It was three months ago." Kendra tried to summon her smile, but gave up when it didn't materialize. She repressed the urge to rub at the nape of her neck, where she was certain every single fine hair was standing at attention. "But I feel certain you know that."

"Indeed."

And something in the way he studied her then made her feel as if she was trembling again, from the inside out. As if her own bones had betrayed her. She had the wild notion that she should leap across the room, slap her hands over his mouth if necessary, do anything she could to keep him from saying whatever it was he'd come here to say… But she didn't.

"Three months," he repeated, as if for emphasis. "And in that time, have you bled?"

She felt all the color and sensation drain from her. "What?"

"It is a simple question, if indelicate. Because we did not use protection, Kendra. And if you have not bled—"

Her pulse was taking over her body, beating *at* her. "Why are we talking about this? How is it your business? And anyway, I moved to a different country. It's not unusual to miss one or two—"

She cut herself off, horrified.

The reality of what she was saying slammed into her anyway, flattening her. And then it was as if she was swallowed up in the ferocious blaze of his glare.

Balthazar did not move. He did not close the space between them.

And still Kendra felt as if he'd lunged at her. Or did she only wish he had?

Did she really long for his touch so much? But she knew the answer to that. She lived it every night.

"Is this your family's latest attempt to force my hand?" Balthazar asked idly, though his gaze was afire with the darkest, harshest condemnation. With a bitter hatred that made her breath hitch. "This will not end for you the way you imagine, Kendra. I promise you that."

CHAPTER SIX

BALTHAZAR'S WORST FEARS had come true.

And he still couldn't quite believe it.

He followed the remote road to the cottage Kendra had said was hers. Which could mean she was letting it, or could mean it was her father's, or could mean, well, anything. He didn't believe a word she said. He didn't believe *her.*

He certainly hadn't believed her flustered response to his appearance earlier. That he would come for her was the point of all this, surely. It was the final move in her game.

Balthazar had been well and truly played. He still couldn't quite accept it, but facts did not wait for his acceptance to be true.

He certainly did not believe that Kendra Connolly wasn't fully aware that they hadn't used protection that night. He imagined she'd been counting down the days, same as him. The fact that she'd taken herself off to a foreign country was evidence enough of her guilt, to his mind.

And he'd been waiting all this time for her to show her hand.

Instead, she'd appeared to first take on the life of a middle-aged expatriate. Pottery and painting and God only knew what other pointless things, the province of the entitled and bored. Then she'd begun waiting tables, of all things, which might have been more age appropriate, but made no sense for the Connolly heiress.

It had to be another part of her game, though he couldn't imagine how it fit.

The road opened up and a cottage came into view. Balthazar gritted his teeth. Because it looked like…a cozy, pastoral scene of Provence. Yellows, blues, and purples. Fields of wildflowers on either side with a humble dwelling on a soft rise, lit up against the darkening summer sky.

He had been anticipating the kind of "cottage" people like Thomas Connolly like to call the gaudy, massive mansions in places like Newport, Rhode Island.

This was not that.

And Balthazar didn't quite know what to do with this unpretentious house. Much less the woman who stood in the open doorway, the buttery light from within making her glow.

Damn her.

Balthazar came to a stop in a cloud of his own bad temper. He slammed out of the car, unfolding his body from the low-slung leather seats and taking longer than necessary to smooth his shirt into place when it did not require smoothing. His clothing did not defy him. It was only this creature before him, standing there like an innocent again, who dared.

"I hope you didn't have any trouble finding this place," she said in that bright, chirpy voice he'd heard earlier at the winery.

He detested it.

"I am capable of using navigation technology, thank you," he growled at her.

Kendra did not back down. She only sighed,

slightly. "I see this is going to be contentious. What a lovely change."

Balthazar did not appreciate her ironic tone of voice.

Because it had been three months of worrying about this very thing. Three months of assuring himself that nothing would come of the one and only time he'd failed to protect himself, his family, and his wealth.

And with a Connolly, to add insult to injury.

Still, his self-delusion might have illuminated his darker moments, but he was a practical man. That, too, had been impressed upon him by his father's heavy hand, whether he liked it or not. He had therefore enlisted a special security detail to track her movements. To see if she would give herself away.

To make sure that whatever happened, he was on hand to intervene if it went in a direction he didn't like.

He'd expected her to head to a clinic in an attempt to draw him out. Her relocation to France had confused him. But perhaps it, too, had been as good as waving a flag—because here he was.

Still, he hadn't been sure.

Not until that performance she'd put on earlier in the kitchen of the winery.

"Perhaps you can explain to me what exactly it is you think you are doing, pretending to be a plucky waitress?" He moved around the front of the sports car and then stayed there, not quite trusting himself to venture any closer to her, which was another personal betrayal. They were adding up. "It does not suit you, *kopéla*. I think you must know this."

She might have seemed happy, but Balthazar could not accept that it was real. It was a role she was playing, nothing more. It was a way to hide from what she'd done, who she was, and what must come next.

Surely she had to know this.

He certainly knew it.

As she was almost certainly carrying his child, this rustic life she'd arranged around her this summer was unacceptable, as she must surely have been aware. The mother of a Skalas heir could not be *in service*, God forbid.

He told himself this supposed happiness of hers had to be fake. It had to be part of the bait in her trap.

There was no other explanation.

She only looked at him for a moment as if *he* was the one who made no sense. It meant there was nothing to do but gaze back at her.

Damn her, but she looked…angelic.

It made him want to break things.

The light from inside the cottage made her hair look strawberry blonde and drenched in gold. That heart-shaped face had haunted him for months now—years, if he was honest—and it was far prettier in person than it had been in his memory.

That infuriated him all the more.

If he didn't know any better, if he chose to rely on all his usual instincts, Balthazar would have been tempted to swear that there wasn't a shred of deceit in this woman.

She was the best manipulator he'd ever seen, he reflected in that moment, as the light exalted her and made her look something like beatific. The apple did not fall far from its gnarled, ugly tree.

He ordered himself to unclench his fists.

"I have to do something with myself," Kendra said quietly. *Thoughtfully*, he would have said, if she was someone else. "It turns out a life of leisure doesn't suit me at all."

"Yet three months ago I could have sworn you were attempting to be some kind of businesswoman. Wasn't that your game?" He could remember that night entirely too well. "That outfit. The bartering."

A kind of shadow moved over her face, and she shrugged. It forced him to pay attention to the fact that she was not dressed like any kind of businesswoman now. She had changed out of the summery shift dress she'd been wearing at the winery and was now dressed simply in a pair of denim jeans and a deep blue tank top with wide shoulder straps that only drew more attention to the elegance of her neck and that clavicle that made his mouth water.

He did not understand how he could want her like this.

Even now.

"My services were not required in the family business," Kendra said.

"Were they not? That sounds like a remarkably antiseptic version of family drama."

Another shadow crossed her pretty face, but this one looked like temper. "What does it matter if it's antiseptic or not? I don't work for the family company. And if I'm not working for the family company, why stay with the family?"

"So your father and your brother, those paragons of virtue—"

"There's no need to overdo it, Balthazar." Her tone was dry. Almost amused, though not quite. "At a certain level, being that sardonic might actually hurt you, don't you think?"

He almost laughed, but caught himself. "They were happy to send you out like a pair of pimps, is that it? But couldn't find it in them to offer you a cubicle tucked away in their offices?"

The color in her cheeks bloomed. "That is…an absolutely revolting way to put it."

"Is it incorrect?"

She made a sound as if she was clearing her throat, then swung around and walked into the cottage.

"I think," she said as she moved, "that this conversation is going to require wine."

Balthazar prowled in behind her, expecting to see…he didn't know what. Something that shouted out her guilt. Something that penetrated this front she put on.

But instead he found himself in an open, bright room that sprawled from the front door into an open kitchen at the back that looked out over a small terrace. There was real art on the walls, placed in a haphazard way that suggested they were there because the owner enjoyed them, not because she was showing off a collection. There were bookshelves and stacks of books and magazines everywhere, but the cottage didn't feel fussy or overstuffed. The overall effect was of a kind of bohemian joy in art and literature.

It didn't fit with his impression of this woman. He found himself frowning at the wide, cozy couches that still held the imprint of her body.

Then he remembered what she'd said as she'd walked inside.

"No wine for you, *kopéla*," he growled.

He closed the front door behind him and watched her closely as she turned, halfway across the airy room. He noticed that her feet were bare, and could not have explained why that poked at him if his life had depended upon it.

Nor could he understand why it very much felt as if it did.

"No wine for me?" She looked baffled. "If you're some kind of teetotaler—"

"Hardly." He waited for her to get his meaning and when she didn't, another surge of fury swept through him. "Have you forgotten you might be pregnant?"

He didn't quite know what to do when she paled, as if she truly had forgotten. When that couldn't be true.

How could that be true?

And because she seemed frozen there, staring at him with her eyes wide and horrified, he moved toward her and tossed the small package he'd brought with him onto an accent table beside her.

She cleared her throat. "Why do I doubt you brought me gifts?"

Balthazar didn't trust himself to speak. But he must have communicated himself all the same, because Kendra moved to the table and picked up the small carrier bag, then blew out a loud breath when she looked inside.

"Wow." She laughed, though he could see from the color on her face and the sudden sheen in her eyes that she didn't find any of this particularly amusing. *Good*, he thought.

"Pregnancy tests. You thought I needed pregnancy tests. Five of them, no less."

"It will do for a start."

She raised her gaze to his and actually had the gall to look shocked. "You can't possibly imagine that I'm going to…"

"Now, please."

His voice was soft, but a command. He saw it move in her, a kind of jolt.

"No." She dropped the carrier bag on the table as if it had fangs. "I will not—"

"Allow me to explain to you what is going

to happen, Kendra." Balthazar didn't move closer to her. He didn't trust himself. Nor did he raise his voice. Even so, she jolted again, harder this time. Her eyes snapped to his and he approved. Maybe now she would take this—*him*—seriously. "I do not know how you intended to play this game. But you chose the wrong man to play it with. I do not believe the innocent act because, lest we forget, I know the truth about you. And even if I did not, I know exactly what your family is capable of."

"I'm not acting. I'm not an actor, and even if I was, I certainly wouldn't bother to put on a performance for a man I never planned to lay eyes on again."

"Silence."

That command sliced straight across the room, and if he wasn't mistaken, straight through her.

Kendra's breathing sounded a little heavy, almost as if she was having an emotional response…

Or, the appropriately cynical part of him chimed in, *she knows she's caught.*

"Your intentions do not matter to me," he told her, harsh and precise so there could be no mistake. "I would prefer to determine, here and now, if you are pregnant. If this nightmare is truly happening."

"I vote no, it's not." She jerked her head toward the door. "Feel free to leave. Now."

"But of course, I do not trust you, Kendra." Balthazar wanted to reach for her and lectured himself, sternly, to keep his hands to himself. This situation could hardly be improved by repeating the same mistake. And besides, he needed to interrogate himself as to why and how he could possibly want this woman the way he did, when he knew what she was. When he knew exactly what she'd done. "Therefore, tomorrow—regardless of what we discovered tonight—we will fly to Athens for an appointment with my personal physician."

He stood there, feeling like an avenging angel, as she gaped at him.

The way an innocent he was railroading might—

But Balthazar dismissed that.

"There is not one part of what you said that's going to happen." Kendra crossed her arms and held herself stiffly. "Not one single part."

"This is nonnegotiable."

"Are you under the impression that I…work for you?" This time, her laugh bordered on the hysterical, and he had to fight—again—the urge to put his hands on her. "The only interest I ever had in you was as an emissary from my family on behalf of my brother. Who, I can't help but notice, you have yet to report to the authorities."

"Was this not the entire point of your little gambit?"

Against his will, against his own orders, he found himself moving closer to her. When he noticed that he'd placed himself within arm's reach, he stopped, but it didn't help.

Nothing helped. This woman was the only addiction Balthazar had ever had, and he would not succumb to it. To her.

He refused.

"There is no gambit," she was saying, her voice hot and her eyes dark. "This is my life.

A life I put together to suit *me*, not anyone else. I don't care what you think of it and I certainly don't appreciate you storming in here like you have some claim—"

"I have every claim."

Balthazar's voice was pure ice.

Kendra made a soft sound that might have been a gasp, as if he'd punctured her straight through. He rather hoped he had.

"Whatever life you think you might have had here, you forfeited your right to it when you involved me," he told her. Ferociously. "You must realize that there exists absolutely no possibility that I will allow you to give birth to my child anywhere that is not under my direct supervision."

"If I'm pregnant," she said, and on some distant level he noticed that she almost stuttered over that word, "I will handle it. My way. It has nothing to do with you."

"I will require genetic testing to determine paternity, obviously. Because oddly, Kendra, I do not trust you."

"Genetic testing…" She blinked, then lifted a hand as if warding him off. "I understand that you take great pride in crashing about the planet, ordering everyone around and taking your revenge when they don't do what you want. But I have already spent a lifetime putting up with that from my actual relatives. I have no intention of allowing you to take up where they left off."

"How will you stop it?" he asked with genuine curiosity, though there was a kind of silken threat in his voice.

He did nothing to hide it.

And he expected her to cower. To look away, keep her eyes downcast, make herself small, the way most of his subordinates and rivals did in his presence.

Instead, Kendra Connolly charged across the few feet remaining between them and actually brandished her finger in his face.

It was…astonishing, not alarming.

Such a thing had never happened before. Not with anyone other than his father, that was.

"You can go straight to hell," Kendra threw at him. "And you can start by getting out of my house."

Balthazar shrugged. "Whether I am in this house or out of it, that will make no difference. The outcome will be the same."

"You have absolutely no authority over me. I don't even *like* you. And even if I did, the state of my womb is none of your business."

"Think again, Kendra."

He saw sheer murder on her face, and something about it…delighted him.

Balthazar had now seen a number of different versions of this woman. The fluttery, overcome, supposed innocent that night in the gazebo. The cool, controlled businesswoman who had sold herself so matter-of-factly and then kissed him like the culmination of a lifetime of his most erotic fantasies. The sunny, happy little waitress at the winery.

And even the woman who had greeted him at the door tonight, seemingly angelic. Bathed in light and not nearly as intimidated by him she ought to have been.

Now there was this version. Unafraid, uncowed, and somehow even more beautiful because of it.

He had come here wanting to do absolutely

nothing but crush her, and instead he found himself hard again. That longing, that impossible need, stormed through him as if it intended to tear him apart.

She had no idea how close he came to simply sweeping her into his arms and tasting her mouth again. To lose himself that completely, that quickly.

No matter what she'd done to him.

This weakness will soon rule you, a voice inside that sounded far too much like his harsh father lashed out at him. *Then you will be no better than she is. Is that what you want?*

His trouble was he knew exactly what he wanted.

Kendra dropped that finger, but only so she could prop her hands on her hips. "You make a lot of threats but I think we both know they're empty. Because this is the modern world, not whatever medieval daydream you have going on."

Balthazar laughed, then. "I would advise you not to make yourself comfortable with that fantasy." He laughed again when she scowled at him. "I would prefer it if you agreed to my terms. I would prefer it if you took those tests now, to spare us both the suspense. But I don't require your agreement or cooperation, *kopéla*. Either way, I will have my answers in the end."

"*Either way?* What are you going to do?" Kendra scoffed at him. "Kidnap me?"

But Balthazar only smiled.

CHAPTER SEVEN

THEY LANDED IN Athens the next morning.

And while Balthazar had not, technically, kidnapped her, he hadn't exactly left her any choice.

Kendra hated herself for not finding a way out of the situation, but she hadn't.

She hadn't—and she wasn't sure she really wanted to ask herself why that was.

Balthazar hadn't bothered to continue arguing with her last night. He'd left her after flashing that enigmatic smile, the one that had made her shiver with foreboding. But before he'd driven off in that absurd sports car of his that she was fairly certain was as bespoke as the clothes he wore, he'd made a quick call in emphatic Greek.

Within moments, two glossy black SUVs had pulled up.

"You called the cavalry?" she'd asked.

He'd smiled again, and it wasn't any better that time. "Insurance, that is all."

"Weird." Kendra had eyed the men who poured out of the SUVs. Balefully. "They look a great deal like your own private army."

"You may call them whatever you like, Kendra," Balthazar had said. "They are not here for you."

"Excellent news. I'll have them make themselves comfortable in the lavender fields while I take myself off to Monaco for the weekend."

"Do as you like." Another, third version of that smile of his made her bones feel cold. "My men will protect my potential heir."

And then he'd taken himself off in that obnoxious car, leaving *his men* behind.

Men who would protect the baby she refused to believe she was carrying, not her.

Kendra had retreated back into the cottage and barricaded herself inside. She'd pulled all the curtains and then had sat there on one of Great-Aunt Rosemary's cozy little couches, very deliberately *not* staring across the room at the sack of pregnancy tests Balthazar had left behind.

She had done nothing but obsessively count days since he'd showed up at the winery. She'd gone over it again and again. The truth was, she hadn't spared a single thought about whether or not her monthly cycle was showing up as it should have been…because she'd never had any reason to think about such things. Not only had Kendra never been late, as far as she knew—she'd never had any reason to worry about it if for some reason she had been.

Why hadn't it occurred to her to worry about it now that there was a reason?

But she knew the answer to that. She might wake in the night, suffused with heat and with Balthazar's name on her lips, but by day she never, ever allowed herself to think about that night. To think about *him.* Part of that was also not thinking about her own body— from the things he'd made her feel to its biological functions.

As she'd sat there in her cottage, barricaded in against truths she didn't want to face, Kendra honestly hadn't known if she'd been motivated by denial...or survival.

Either way, the longer she'd stared at that bag full of pregnancy tests, the more it seemed to overtake the room, crowding out the books and the art Great-Aunt Rosemary had left behind. And the more it seemed directly connected to the panic inside of her, pounding at her, filling her up like a wicked flood.

Until she couldn't breathe.

And so it was that Kendra discovered that she really was pregnant with Balthazar Skalas's child while hiding in the small bathroom of her great-aunt's cottage after midnight, hiding from the men he'd sent to make sure she stayed there, *after* making implicit kidnapping threats.

She'd taken all five tests, sure that they had to be defective. That the next one would prove that she wasn't actually living through...this.

But they all showed her the exact same thing.

Kendra was pregnant.

And when she finally stopped chugging water so she could make a new test happen, when she finally accepted that no new test was going to change the truth…the whole world shifted.

With such a dramatic, irrevocable jolt that she'd found herself on the floor of the bathroom, her back against the wall, staring at the incontrovertible evidence before her.

Five times over.

She'd remembered that night in his office vividly. Too vividly, really, when she now knew what would become of it.

Had she been so quick to pretend nothing had happened because it had been so…raw? She was an educated, sophisticated woman who not only had not inquired about protection, she'd never given it a moment's thought, afterward. It had never occurred to her that anything like this could happen.

And as she'd huddled there on the cool bathroom floor, she'd had to face a number of realities. Including the fact that she'd tried her hardest to blank out what had happened in New York because it hadn't been anything like the fantasies of him she'd carried around in her head after encountering him in that gazebo. It had been so much more...*physical*. Each and every sensation so intense she still wasn't sure if it had been pain or pleasure—only that she wanted more. She didn't have a single memory or feeling about Balthazar Skalas that wasn't complicated. Complex.

When she'd been taught again and again that sex was no place for tangled emotions and overwhelming memories. It was meant to be a lovely, celebratory thing, that was all. Not an experience so darkly erotic that she could only face it fast asleep.

"Daylight is no place for unpleasant things, dear," her mother had always said.

Kendra had only realized then, curled up on the floor, that she'd taken that to heart. Maybe a bit too much to heart. Because she'd been living her whole life like this, hadn't she? Her head so far in the sand she was surprised she could breathe through it.

The last few months had been nothing more or less than the inevitable conclusion of a lifetime of her own ostrich impression. She'd ignored the obvious indicators that her father was always the kind of man who would send his own daughter off to *appeal to Balthazar as a man*. She'd ignored the unpleasant reality that he supported Tommy, who was by no definition a good man. She'd ignored everything that didn't suit her.

Maybe it wasn't a surprise that she'd ignored what was happening in her own body, too.

She'd sat there, her knees pulled beneath her chin, too stunned by her own stupidity to even bother crying about it.

That would come later, Kendra had suspected. She could almost feel an emotional breakdown hovering there like a storm, just out of reach over the horizon.

But first she could do nothing but marvel at her own naivete.

Balthazar was upsettingly correct. Her own family had pimped her out.

And it wasn't as if *he* was much better. She could feel the hatred in him. He seethed with it. He hated her brother. He detested her father.

Much as some part of her didn't wish to think about it, he was no fan of hers, either.

And still she had marched herself into that office building, a lamb to the slaughter— though in her case, she'd actually believed she was some kind of wolf, not a lamb at all.

But now it was all worse.

So much worse, Kendra didn't truly understand how she was going to live through whatever came next.

She'd spent her whole life trying to be perfect, and instead, she'd gone and gotten herself knocked up the first time she'd so much as touched a man. It was her parents' worst nightmare, as they'd made clear a thousand times while she was growing up. Her mother might very well slip off into a coma, so appalled was Emily Connolly sure to be at this news.

That was bad enough. Far worse was the trepidation she could feel churn about inside her as she tried to imagine how on earth she was going to navigate *sharing a child* with a man like Balthazar when she wasn't sure she could survive sharing a car ride with him.

She'd actually laughed out loud, there in

her bathroom, then winced at how unhinged she sounded.

"I'm sorry," she'd whispered, sneaking her hands over her belly, though it still seemed impossible to her that there could be a life inside. A *life*. A baby. *My baby*, something in her whispered. "I'll find a way, don't worry."

Because Balthazar Skalas might be his own level of impossible, but Kendra had no intention of hiding from reality any longer. She was going to be a mother. She was not going to be *her* mother.

She'd never been any good at fighting for herself, but she would fight for this child.

"No matter what," she'd promised the tiny life growing inside her, there on the bathroom floor and a few more times in her bed, too, for good measure.

But the next morning, far too early for someone who'd stayed up as late as she had, Balthazar had been pounding at her door, and Kendra had made a decision on the spot that there was no point fighting him. Probably because she knew he would win. And she really didn't want to see how, exactly, he would go about physically removing her from France.

She'd seen no reason to share the news with him. He could wait for the ill-gotten gains of his kidnapping attempt to learn what she already knew. If he marinated in his temper while he waited, all the better.

He'd stood there in the cottage's main room, a thundercloud of fury as she'd moved about collecting items like her passport and her great-aunt's oversize scarf that she could fling about her neck and pretend was a fashion accessory when really, it was more like a portable blanket she planned to use to soothe herself.

Because if the look on Balthazar's face had been any guide, Kendra was going to need some soothing.

He'd driven her to a private airfield outside of Nice without a word. The flight had been short and equally silent.

The tension between them was so thick it seemed to settle on Kendra like smog.

Once in Athens, Balthazar herded her off the plane and into yet another astonishingly glossy and aspirational sports car, then drove her into the center of the ancient city itself.

"I'm astonished," she managed to say when he stopped before what looked like an indistinguishable block of flats. "I would have thought that the mighty Balthazar lived on his own mountaintop. In an appropriate castle. With *several* moats."

"This is a medical facility," he clipped out, sounding bored and impatient. "And this is a private entrance."

He parked the car at the behest of a set of overawed attendants, then marched her into an elevator. She was whisked up to a series of private rooms, a waiting area and then an exam room, and Balthazar only glared stonily at her when she dared to suggest she might like some privacy.

"Really," she tried. "I would prefer it."

His mouth curved into that hard line. "This is no time for fantasies, Kendra."

When it was done, both pregnancy and paternity had been determined.

Kendra felt the truth like a stone, heavy and unwieldy, crushing her even when she stood upright. Balthazar, meanwhile, had transformed from a mere thunderstorm to the threat of a far more terrifying tornado, evident in the blazing fury she could see in his dark eyes.

The trip back to that offensively bright car of his was so tense that she found herself shaking.

"Balthazar," she began as he roared his way out of the parking area and back into the crowded streets of Athens, "I really think—"

"If you have any sense of self-preservation whatsoever," he growled, an imposing fury beside her as he drove, "you will be quiet."

The ferocity in his words left her winded.

Kendra decided self-preservation was an excellent idea and stayed silent for the rest of the drive. It was a short one, ending at another private entrance to a corporate parking area and another gleaming elevator. Where he ushered her, in that same grim silence, up to the roof of an office building she only belatedly realized was the corporate headquarters of Skalas & Sons. Where a helicopter waited to carry them off.

She could have argued, she supposed. Thrown a fit on the rooftop, where there were no witnesses but Balthazar's men and the ancient city spread out beneath them. She could at least have *tried*.

But she didn't see how fighting a losing battle with a tornado was going to help either her or her baby.

Her baby.

Kendra might hate herself for her weaknesses when this was all said and done, but for the moment, she wrapped her arms around the middle she'd thought was expanding thanks to eating her way through Provence and sat with that. She was having a baby.

His baby.

And when they landed on a small island surrounded by a gleaming blue sea, she didn't have it in her to make smart remarks about castles or moats. Because the island was not large. There was no sign of anything like a village. There was one sprawling house on the higher end of the island, a collection of outbuildings, and beaches.

She supposed most people would consider it paradise, but she knew better.

It was a prison.

Balthazar marched off into the sprawling villa, a celebration of Greek architecture with wide-open spaces that flowed in and out of the outdoors. Letting in the sea and sky from every angle.

Kendra followed him because what else was she to do? Attempt to fly herself back to the mainland?

"There is a skeleton staff on the island," he informed her when he led her to a bedroom that sat above the sea and then stood there, glowering at her, as if she'd impregnated herself purely to spite him. It occurred to her that he thought she had. "They'll operate according to the orders of the housekeeper, Panagiota, who has been with my family since my father was young and is deeply loyal to me. You may assume that anything she says comes directly from me."

"You're leaving me here?" Kendra should have assumed that was what he was doing, she knew. She had the absurd thought that if she'd known she wouldn't be returning to the cottage, she would have packed more of her things. As if *her things* were what mattered at the moment. "For how long?"

He took a long while to simply *look* at her, as if he was trying to see beneath her skin. As if he was looking for something. "For as long as it takes."

She tried to gather herself. "You are aware, I hope, that there's a specific timeline? And we're in the second trimester. Leaving only one remaining."

"I can count." His tone was withering.

"Are you really planning to leave me here for *six months?*"

But even as she asked the question, she knew the answer. She was glad she'd wrapped her great-aunt's gauzy scarf around her on the helicopter ride. It felt like a hug.

"Consider this a kindness," Balthazar bit off. "There's nothing I have to say to you right now that you would like to hear, I promise you."

"Right," she managed to say, trying to find her feet beneath her. Trying to remind herself that no matter how intimidating she found him, and no matter how beautiful, this wasn't only about the two of them any longer. "Because when we had sex with each other and were both present and accounted for *in your office*, only I was scheming. You were nothing but a naive maiden, lost in the woods."

"Do not test me, Kendra." His voice was something like a whisper, though lethal. She could feel it pierce her like a blade. She gripped the scarf around her even more tightly. "You will not like how I handle you. How I address what you have done to me. Let me promise you this."

"You can't really think I'm going to quietly remain here." She shook her head at him. "I have a life, Balthazar. One I made all for myself, no matter what you might think of it. I have—"

"If you wished to have a life, you should not have irrevocably changed mine."

He moved closer then, towering over her, and she could see a stark ferocity in his gaze that should have terrified her. Instead, something in her longed to meet it. Rise up on her toes, tilt her head, and—

Well. It wasn't as if she was unaware of her own issues. There was that.

"Perhaps it's escaped your notice," she said, hoping the things she longed for so foolishly weren't written all over her face, but mine is the life that is already changed. Mine is the life you decided to alter in more ways than one. I'm the one carrying this baby. I'm the one you've carted all over Europe today, and apparently plan to leave behind on this island."

"The life you knew is over." She watched as a muscle clenched in his jaw. "I suspect this was your plan from the start. I must congratulate you. I did not see it coming."

"Yes," she snapped at him, "I decided that I would miraculously become pregnant, the way all women do. That's why there is no such thing as fertility issues. All women *decide*, and then do it."

He made a sound she could only describe as a growl, but she didn't slink away. Something in her *thrilled* to the sound. She kept her gaze steady and forced her knees to remain strong beneath her.

"You may have saved your brother after all," Balthazar said in that quiet way of his that made the world shake around him. "But I promise you, Kendra. You will live to regret this."

For a moment she thought—*wished?*—that those big, hard hands of his were going to reach out to her. Take hold of her.

Touch her the way he did in her dreams, night after night—

But instead, Balthazar turned on his heel and stalked away from her.

Kendra stayed where she was, shaken so deeply by her own longing, even now, that she was surprised she didn't sink to the floor. Was it self-hatred that made her tremble? Or was it that impossible yearning that she couldn't stamp out?

And then she had to force herself not to panic, somehow, when she heard the helicopter's rotors. When Balthazar disappeared into the sky, leaving her behind with these things she knew about herself now.

The worst of them being that no matter what he did, she still wanted him.

It took Kendra a solid ten days to investigate every single nook and cranny of the house and each of the outbuildings, desperate to find something she could use to make her escape.

There had been nothing. Panagiota was kind enough, but firm. She apologized repeatedly, but changed nothing. There was no cell service. Certainly no internet. At least, not any that Kendra was permitted to access.

Though she had to face the fact that even if there was, she had no idea who she would call. Her family would be delighted that she was in a position to bargain further with Balthazar. They would do nothing to help her.

Kendra took it as a mark of her personal growth that she knew this now.

The same way she knew, when she'd finished marching around the small island looking for boats to the mainland, that the real truth was worse.

She didn't want to leave.

She wanted Balthazar to come back.

The way she knew he would, because no matter how angry he might have been, she was carrying his child.

Maybe what she did looked like surrender, but Kendra rather thought she was conserving her strength for the real fight—which certainly wasn't the quietly insistent Panagiota, who was, after all, only doing Balthazar's bidding.

She ate what he wanted her to eat, according to the nutritional guide he'd apparently left with the housekeeper. There was no way off the island—and she'd looked—so she took long, rambling walks on the beaches, over the fields, and through the groves of olive trees.

She slept in the bed he'd told her was hers, and even though he wasn't there, she felt the imprint of him as if he truly was holding her where he wanted her.

"By the neck," she muttered to herself one morning.

But she knew that wasn't quite right. She knew it was quite a bit lower.

One week passed, then another. Summer

began to wane, though on a Greek island in the Aegean it was hard to note the difference.

Balthazar did not contact her. His messages were sent through Panagiota. They were always terse and to the point, and still, Kendra was sure she could feel the gathering storm of his temper from across the sea.

She heard the rotors first on an afternoon six weeks after he'd left her. She was curled up in her favorite spot, a swinging chair out on one of the terraces, the sun in her face and a book in her lap from the library she'd been reading her way through.

Kendra felt a kind of electricity shoot through her at the sound. She sat up, aware that if she squinted, this prison of hers bore a distinct resemblance to what she might have considered paradise when she was younger. Nothing to do but take long walks on a secluded beach and lie about reading books? She should have been delirious with joy.

Sometimes she forgot that she wasn't. That she'd been imprisoned here, no matter how pretty it was.

That she was pregnant with the child of a man who detested her.

A man whose memory woke her in the night, still, on fire with need.

Kendra stayed where she was. She kept on gazing down at her book, even when she heard the faint sound of footsteps against the stones behind her.

And she would have known it was Balthazar even if he hadn't made a sound. She could feel the leading edge of the storm. She could feel the wind snapping at her, the temperature drop, and far off, she was certain, the warning rumble of thunder.

She should have been scared. Instead, what charged around inside her felt a lot more like exhilaration.

"What a pretty picture you make," came his sardonic, insulting voice. Darker than she recalled, maybe. But still, it arrowed straight to her core, making her melt. That easily. "What a shame that I know it is all lies."

Kendra wanted to hurl the book she was reading at his head.

Somehow, she refrained.

"How nice of you to stop in, Balthazar," she said calmly instead. "You do know, don't you, that pregnancies keep going even if you'd prefer to pretend that they don't? I mention this because eventually, when you deign to make an appearance, I won't be the only one here."

"The doctor is even now setting up an exam room in one of the guest bedrooms. He will perform a full examination."

"A prison infirmary," she replied gaily. "What a treat."

Kendra looked at him then and she wished she hadn't.

Because looking at Balthazar…hurt.

He looked like exactly who and what he was. The devil, one of the richest men alive, and her enemy.

All wrapped up in that brooding, near brutal intensity and a dark, bespoke suit that proclaimed his power to the whole of the Mediterranean.

If he was less beautiful, would she be less… thrown?

It shouldn't matter how beautiful he is, she

snapped at herself. *It should only matter that he's locked you away on this island.*

"I don't know why you bothered to come," she continued, keeping her voice brighter than it should have been. "At this point, wouldn't it be easier if you just stayed away? I can raise your child in shame and solitude all by myself."

"I doubt you feel anything approaching shame," he said, with one of those hard laughs that nearly made her shiver, though she sat in the sunshine. "And it is of no matter, anyway. I have no intention of leaving you here forever, no matter how tempting the prospect. Like it or not, you will be the mother of my child. And I am Balthazar Skalas. There are certain conventions that need to be followed."

"I can't imagine what you mean. More kidnaps? More insults and accusations? I can hardly wait."

His smile then was wintry. It made something cold and bright flash over her, worse than before.

"Why, Kendra. I thought you knew."

That he seemed to be enjoying himself made her shudder, and she knew he saw it.

He thinks he's beaten me, Kendra thought, and found she was holding her breath.

"I've come to congratulate you, of course," Balthazar told her. His dark eyes gleamed with satisfaction. Worse, with triumph. "As we are to be married tomorrow."

CHAPTER EIGHT

IT WAS ALMOST worth the fact that Balthazar was marrying her against his will, if at his command, to see that stunned look on Kendra's face.

Better still, a flash of temper besides, proving she wasn't nearly as calm or collected as she sometimes acted.

Balthazar almost slipped and showed her how much her reaction pleased him, but caught himself just in time. She didn't deserve to see his own responses, but why should he be the only person dreading the inevitable? She was a Connolly, she had conspired against him from the start with her vile father and brother, and this was her fault.

He ignored the voice inside him that reminded him that her conspiracies could not have gained any ground had he not lost his head completely and sampled her without protecting himself. The way he'd been ignoring that voice for weeks.

But he didn't like to think about that. He was appalled that he'd lost control of himself so utterly, when his father had spent long years teaching him how to strip any and all emotions out of every last moment and situation. Even sex was meant to be a release, nothing more.

Nothing...overwhelming.

He wrestled himself back under control. As he should have done from the start.

"I will not be marrying you," she shot back at him, predictably. She bristled in her hanging chair and he watched dispassionately as she struggled to pull herself out of its embrace, then stood. Rather rounder than the last time he'd seen her, though he refused to focus on that. On what her fuller figure meant. "Not tomorrow. Not ever."

"You're beginning to bore me," he replied, almost idly, and knew he sounded sterner than perhaps he'd intended when she stiffened. "You will not do this, you will not do that. I suggest you come up with a new song. In the meantime, the doctor is waiting."

"What magical powers I must possess that I can bore you in six seconds after your absence of six *weeks*. Maybe the problem is your attention span."

Balthazar did not lower himself to sniping with her, especially because he wanted to do just that. He gestured toward the archway that led into the house and waited for her to obey him.

For a moment, he wasn't sure what she would do. Refuse? Fight him? Worse, he wasn't entirely sure what *he* planned to do if she did either of those things. Nor could he read the expressions that chased each other across her lovely, flushed face when she swept past him, though he got the overall impression of feminine fury.

She would be his wife come the morning. She was carrying his child.

She was his enemy.

All good reasons not to want her with that greedy, driving need that had gotten him into this mess in the first place. And yet Balthazar had to order himself to stand down. To keep his hands to himself. To stop himself before he made this unfortunate situation worse.

He, who could stare down the most powerful men alive and make them regret catching his eye, could barely control himself in the presence of a woman who should have disgusted him.

It was an outrage and it never eased. Three years hadn't dulled his reaction. Why had he assured himself six weeks would do the trick this time?

Balthazar had no answer. Instead, once inside, he led her down the long, bright hallway, across an interior courtyard covered in pink bougainvillea, then ushered her into the set of rooms his staff had rearranged so they could stand in for a medical suite.

And because he knew his doctor would report to him in full, he left her there.

Though he would have died before admitting it, and by his own hand, he was happy for the breathing room.

Because the truth was that Balthazar had been utterly unprepared for the sight of her.

The glow he'd seen in France and had attributed to the lighting at her cottage—or the glory of the Côte d'Azur itself—was worse now. Or better, more like. She was a gleaming, bright and shining thing, and he had no idea how he was meant to cope.

He stood out in the courtyard, surrounded by flowers and the pitiless Aegean sky, and thought of her new *roundness.* The widening of her hips, the swell of her belly. He found he was wholly moved by the knowledge that she carried his child. *His child* tucked inside that beautiful, gently rounded body of hers.

He hadn't expected that. This… insane response to her. A tenderness he abhorred mixed in with too much pounding, bone-rattling *need.*

Tenderness was anathema to him. Softness of any kind led to desperate places—didn't he know that already?

But he refused to think about his own family. Of the things sentimentality had wrought.

There was no need to think of it when he knew who to blame.

Balthazar had convinced himself that his

response to Kendra had been nothing more than two strange moments in time, bookending three years. But it was over now, surely. He'd spent the past month handling the details of what needed to happen next, now that his heir's birth was imminent. Up to and including a meeting with his brother to lay out the changes he would be making in his will and various trusts. For dynastic purposes.

"Kendra... *Connolly*?" Constantine had asked lazily. He had gazed at his brother as he'd lounged about in his typical state of seeming dishevelment all over Balthazar's sleek, modern furniture. Then he'd waved a languid hand at Athens outside the windows as if he expected the whole of Greece to rise up to support his astonishment. "You cannot be serious."

"I would hardly make such announcements in jest."

"She is a Connolly."

"A fact that does not become less appalling the more you repeat it, brother."

Constantine had shaken his head. "What can you possibly be thinking? After everything—" He'd stopped then. The canny look that Balthazar sometimes thought only he had ever seen changed his brother's face. Constantine suddenly looked every inch the shark he was. "Let me guess. You got her pregnant. Good god, Balthazar. How could you be so careless?"

"A simple *congratulations* would do. As you will shortly become an uncle."

Constantine had let out a bark of laughter. "Never let it be said you are not prepared to think outside the box when it comes to taking revenge on our enemies. I am inspired, truly."

And he'd smiled in a way that had distracted Balthazar for a moment, wondering who his brother considered worthy of enemy status—and a revenge scenario to match. He did not fancy that person's chances against the wolf-in-playboy's-clothing Constantine played up for public consumption.

"Prepare yourself," Balthazar had advised his brother that night. "You will be the *koumbaro*."

If Constantine had any further feelings about taking his place at his brother's side in the traditional role of *koumbaro*, combining best man, future godparent, and witness in one, he had wisely kept that to himself.

Possibly too busy concocting his own form of revenge, Balthazar had thought then.

Now Balthazar waited in a riot of blooms and his body's greedy responses to the enemy he planned to take as his wife, forced to remind himself that revenge was the point of this. Revenge had always been the point.

It was simply taking rather a different form than he'd expected it would when Kendra had asked for that appointment with him months back.

He had never imagined how close a Connolly would come to ruining *him*.

Do not allow temptation to change your path, he told himself dourly, despite the sunshine and the bright explosion of pink flowers all around him. *Stay the course.*

And later—after the doctor had announced that Kendra and the baby she carried could not have been in better health, then left them to an evening meal out on one of the terraces over the sea—Balthazar did not bother to wait for the good food or a full belly to dull her temper. He shouldn't have cared what mood she was in. He slid the folder he'd brought for her across the table.

"What is this?" Her voice was clipped. It was at odds with that glow she had about her, and Balthazar disliked it, but he tapped his finger against the thick file anyway.

"These are the agreements that require your signature."

She sniffed, poking at the food on her plate with rather more violence than strictly necessary, to his mind. "I will not be signing anything."

"That does not sound like the new song I suggested you sing," he said, mildly enough. He studied her mutinous expression. "Was I unclear?"

Balthazar expected her to argue with him. If he was honest, he was looking forward to it. Though he wasn't certain he truly wished to acknowledge that what kicked around inside of him was more of that anticipation and hunger than the righteous fury he would have said was guiding his every word and deed.

There was something about this woman that got under his skin. That was the sad truth, no matter how he fought against it. Any hope he might have had that she had released her grip on him in the time he'd spent away from her had disappeared the moment he'd seen her curled up in a chair with the sunlight in her hair, turning it to flame.

Maybe it was time to admit it to himself.

But Kendra didn't make it easy on him. She didn't leap into the fray. Instead, she looked away, her gaze off toward the blue line of the horizon, far in the distance. He imagined she was dreaming of ways to escape him, to avoid the consequences he had been forced to accept.

He resented it.

"I have no interest in your money," she said after a moment, as if studying the inevitable way the sun dipped toward the edge of the world. "You know full well I have my own. There is no need whatsoever to sign agreements to that effect."

"You mean you have your father's money," Balthazar corrected her, sitting back in his chair and absolutely not giving in to his temper. Just because she got to him, it didn't mean he had to lose his grip. He was furious it was even in question. "That is not quite the same thing, is it?"

Her gaze shifted back to him, glittering hot and gold. "Remind me, whose money is it that you were given?"

He found himself smiling. Almost. "Fair point. Though, unlike me, I am unaware of any great financial ventures you've been involved in on your own since you came of age. Please enlighten me."

"I was happily working in a winery in Provence until six weeks ago."

Balthazar lifted a brow. "Are you so divorced from reality that you imagine waiting tables is a wealth-building exercise? Unless, of course, you went about getting your tips in the same way you approached your business meeting with me?"

Kendra didn't rise to the bait and surely he should not have felt a vague sense of disappointment at that.

She sighed as if *he* was the trial. "Surely

the man who has spirited me away to his very own private island is not really speaking to me about *reality*."

And he, who had a cutting response for everything, found he had nothing.

Worse, he found himself sitting there, seething, while Kendra returned her attention to the grilled chicken on her plate, helping herself to more fresh greens from the bowl at her elbow. Ignoring him, he was forced to conclude.

Ignoring him.

Ignoring *him*.

He ordered himself to stop gritting his teeth.

"If I am brutally honest—"

"That would be a bracing shift, I'm sure," she murmured aridly.

Balthazar ignored that. And continued, with great magnanimity. "I am not worried about you, *kopéla*. Obviously it is your father and brother and their grasping, deceitful behavior who concern me more."

"Are you marrying all three of us?"

He couldn't quite read that tone she'd used,

but he could see the look on her face all too well. He couldn't say he liked it.

"Oh, I see," she said when he didn't reply. "I forgot that I am no more than a tool my father and brother alike use for their own nefarious ends. You think you're taking their little toy away and making it yours instead. Naturally you want me to sign documents to enshrine these playground antics into contract law. After all, what could be the harm? This was never my life in the first place."

It was the bitterness in her tone, the harsh slap of it, that got to him then. Balthazar felt as if he'd lost something when she reached out, grabbed the folder, and pulled it toward her.

A feeling that only worsened as she rifled through the pages, signing her name with dramatic flourish.

"You do not appear to be reading the documents, Kendra."

"Does it matter?" She didn't look up at him. "Surely the object of this humiliation is the mere fact of it. Not what the papers actually *say*."

She capped the pen, closed the folder again, and then shoved it all back across the table toward him. "Here you go, Balthazar. Congratulations, you have dominion over me and legal documents to prove it. What a glorious environment this will be for your child."

Balthazar told himself it was the mention of the child that got to him then, that was all. Imagining that child torn between warring parents the way he and his brother had been. He told himself that was all it was.

He had been so focused on the fact of Kendra's pregnancy. What it meant in financial and practical terms. What he was going to have to do to contain the damage and attempt to repair this mistake of his own making.

Somehow, he hadn't thought about the fact his child would be an individual, a whole human being who would grow and laugh—and want his parents to be better, as he had—until now.

It felt a great deal like a kick to the gut.

For a moment, he almost dared imagine what things might have been like if his parents had been different. If they had actually gotten better instead of worse. If they had somehow managed not to poison everything they touched—

But that felt uncomfortably disloyal.

He shoved it aside—aware that it seemed harder to do than it should have.

"Why are you staring at me?" Kendra asked after a while, and he wondered if she found the silence between them oppressive. Or if that was only him, again. "It is not going to change anything."

"Nothing needs to change." He shrugged, no longer feeling oppressed. Not when she was aiming that baleful glare of hers his way. "We will marry in the morning. Though as a Connolly you certainly do not deserve such consideration, you will become my wife. You may thank me."

"I would be happier with less consideration, actually. No thanks required."

"Too bad." His mouth curved into something hard. "The child you carry will be my heir, and I insist any child of mine be legitimate. If you had read the documents you signed, you would know that I have made generous accommodation for you *because* you are the mother of this child, no matter what our future holds."

Somehow, he knew she was not likely to thank him for that, either.

"Do we have a future?" she asked instead. Then frowned. "Or, wait. Do you mean a succession of creative imprisonments for me to enjoy?"

"That is up to you, Kendra."

"Why do I find that very hard to believe?"

Balthazar studied her. "This role you keep attempting to play, that of the wronged innocent, does not suit you."

"Whereas the role of overly controlling bastard seems to fit you perfectly. Almost as if you've had practice. I'm betting you have."

"You have only a few months left." It was a warning, not that Balthazar expected her to take it on board. "Indulge your bitterness as you wish. Once the child is born, it stops. Or I will make certain you see as a little of him as possible."

"I don't know what makes you think it's going to be a boy, aside from wishful thinking," she said, when he'd thought she would have reacted more dramatically to his other threat. She lifted a brow. "And you can try to separate me from this baby. But I wouldn't advise it."

The sun had dropped almost to the sea then. The sky was bathed in golds and reds, a commotion of flame and fury, just like Kendra.

He hated that he'd made that connection.

"Perhaps you are laboring under some misapprehension," he said softly. "I am Balthazar Skalas and we are in Greece. There is no court in the land that would concern itself with your position should I make mine clear."

To his surprise, all she did was laugh. "All these threats. Is this how you're used to interacting with the world? Is this what it's like to be your mistress? No wonder you go through them like tissues."

"This is nothing like being one of my mistresses," he replied silkily, because this was steadier ground. "As that role is far more... active."

Kendra leaned forward and propped her elbows on the table, very much as if she thought she was in a classroom of some kind. "Tell me more about this active mistress lifestyle of yours. Is this going to be a part of my humiliation at your hands? Will I sit, tucked away in this or that luxurious prison, while you prance around with your various women in public places?"

She did not look particularly upset at that possibility, which Balthazar found he disliked. Intensely. "What business is that of yours?"

"I don't ask for myself," Kendra said, aiming that cool smile at him that he remembered too well from his office. "It's your child who concerns me. Then again, perhaps you are not concerned that she will grow up loathing you. Detesting the way you treat her mother and worse, how you humiliate your family in public. But then, wasn't your father that kind of man? Perhaps your child can hope for no better."

It was such a kill shot, aimed so perfectly and with such lethal accuracy, that Balthazar almost laughed. He hadn't seen it coming. In truth, he hadn't imagined she'd had it in her.

That was what he got for assuming she was nothing but a pawn.

He found himself sitting back in his chair, tempted to check to see if he was bleeding.

And as he did, she carried on eating, as if she hadn't a single care in the world.

As if she hadn't lacerated him like that.

"Both of my parents had affairs," he said, eventually.

It was true enough, though it was not an accurate summation of his parents' marriage. Much less what had become of it.

"Demetrius Skalas did not have affairs." Kendra sounded almost placid. Matter-of-fact. "An affair suggests that there were some attempts to keep the behavior undercover. Your father preferred to parade around with a new woman on his arm whenever possible, publicly and horribly. When your mother responded in kind, he divorced her."

"Thank you for reciting facts about which you know nothing," Balthazar managed to grit out, while his pulse pounded at him.

"These are not my facts." She smiled at him, a little more edgily that her calm tone would suggest. "Panagiota may have banned me from the internet, but it turns out that the family housekeeper has a great many facts at her disposal. And is only too happy to share them."

Balthazar shook his head. And tamped down on the urge in him to lash out. Because she wasn't any old adversary. She wasn't her own father, that despicable man. She was the mother of his child, whether he liked it or not. And he was still trying to decide how best to come to terms with that.

"My father was a man of absolutes," he said when the silence between them grew too heavy again. "I do not expect you to understand, but he had strict expectations. And should anyone fall short of those expectations, the consequences were severe. Anyone who knew him knew this."

"Are you saying that your mother earned her humiliation?" Kendra made a face. "I suppose I'd better watch my step."

"I am not my father."

And Balthazar was surprised at how…raw that sounded.

"Are you not?" Kendra sat back, one hand moving to cover her belly. He wanted to decry the theatrics, but he had the strangest notion that it was an unconscious gesture.

Again, he was struck by the fact that *his son* was in there. That *his son* would be out in this same world in a matter of months, calling Balthazar father. Maybe that was why he did not reply to Kendra in the thunderous manner he could have.

The way he should have.

"My brother and I were born in quick succession," he told her instead, because that was also true. "And my mother... After my brother came, I am told, she disappeared. She left us in the care of our nannies and never left her rooms. After that had gone on for some time, my father had her admitted to a private hospital in Austria, where she was better cared for. But she did not return to us for several years."

"And you think that is...evidence against her?"

"It is simply what happened."

"It sounds like you're describing postpartum depression, Balthazar. It wasn't her choice." Kendra studied his face for a moment. "You know that, don't you?"

"What I know is that my father could not abide weakness," Balthazar told her, his voice rough. "In anyone."

Kendra was sitting much too still, that hand still resting on her belly. "So what you're telling me is that your poor mother suffered from a terrible depression and your father took it upon himself to punish her for a chemical and hormonal imbalance that wasn't her fault."

"He was an unforgiving man."

"And what about you?" Kendra asked quietly. "Are you forgiving?"

This was the right time to tell her the rest of it, to see once and for all what she knew and what game she was playing. But somehow, Balthazar couldn't bring himself to do it.

He couldn't stop thinking of a small boy with his eyes, looking at him the way he'd tried to implore his father. Before he'd learned the folly of such things.

Kendra reached over and tapped the folder that still sat there between them. "It would appear that no, you are not particularly forgiving."

"Do you deserve forgiveness, Kendra?" he growled at her, keeping himself still in his chair when he wanted nothing more than to rage. To break things. To hurl the table between them into the sea far below.

Because that was easier than confronting what was happening in him. He thought of his mother, messier and messier throughout his childhood until his father had divorced her. She had gone off to lick her wounds—in horribly public ways. Balthazar had always considered it a defection. He had always judged her, harshly, as much for her particular extramarital affair neither his father nor he could overlook as for her departure.

What he had never done was question how and why she had lost his father's respect in the first place. Much less whether or not that had been fair to her. And he didn't much care for the heavy ball of something like dread that sat in him now he was doing just that.

Thinking about forgiveness didn't help.

"By your reckoning, no," Kendra replied,

but she didn't look particularly broken up about whether or not he might forgive her. As if a lifetime of his father's brand of consequences was right up her alley, when he knew better. He knew what it did to soft creatures like her, didn't he? "But then, I don't need to prove myself to you, Balthazar. I don't care what you believe. I'm going to marry you, not because you've demanded it, but because I'm a rational person who can see that marrying you will afford my child her best possible life. You keep talking about the past if it makes you feel better. I'm focused on the future."

She stood up then, still outrageously graceful despite her fuller figure and her new, big bump. He told himself it was sheer temper that pounded through him. Sheer, unmitigated fury—because what else could it be? What else would he allow it to be?

He was rising before he meant to move, blocking her path.

She stared up at him, her chin lifted as her copper-burnished hair flowed around her, backlit by the setting sun.

"You have no moral high ground here," he

gritted out at her. He wanted to put his hands on her, so he did, gripping her shoulders as he held her before him. "You've achieved what you wanted, but I assure you, the price you pay will be steep."

"What I *wanted*," she threw right back at him, "was peace. Quiet. A cottage all my own filled with books and a fire and as many buttery croissants as I could eat. Which, it turns out, is a great many croissants. Instead you stormed in and carried me off to this place. And I'm not an idiot, Balthazar. I'm not *divorced from reality*. I'm perfectly aware that as prisons go, this one is charming. Beautiful. Some people would dream of coming here and staying here forever. But I'm not one of them."

"If I was interested in what you wanted, Kendra, I would have asked you."

He expected her to recoil at that. To react as if he'd slapped her. Instead, she surged up onto her toes, bringing herself even closer to him.

Exhibiting, he couldn't help but notice, absolutely no fear.

He couldn't think of a single reason that should have made him want her so desperately.

"You can issue all the orders you like," she told him in a rush. "You will never control me. If I happen to go along with your wishes, you can be sure it's because I want to. Not because you told me to."

He managed—just—not to sneer. "From a girl who was willing to prostitute herself at her father's command."

"You don't know anything about my family," she threw right back at him. "Or about me. And I don't want you to know. You don't deserve it."

She was so bright with her own outrage. Alight with self-righteous indignation, and Balthazar should have found that laughable. He told himself he did.

But he didn't laugh.

Instead, he jerked her toward him and set his mouth to hers.

At last.

And it was that same wild, impossible fire. That same electric explosion, as if he'd been struck by lightning—yet he wanted more. Always and ever more.

He angled his head to one side, taking the kiss deeper and growling his appreciation when she met him, all slick heat and greed.

And he was amazed, again, to find his head spinning when she pushed herself away.

"Kissing me changes nothing," she managed to say, though he took perhaps too much pride in the fact her voice shook. "Do you really think that a kiss like that is any kind of punishment at all? Here's a news flash. It's not. If I didn't like it, I would bite you."

"Yes, yes, *kopéla*," he drawled, suddenly enjoying himself when she scowled at him. "You're very fierce. You have fangs, and I promise you, I cannot wait to feel them on my skin."

Kendra bared her teeth at him and he laughed, he wanted her so intensely. So comprehensively it was like pain. But he knew pain. He knew how to live with it. In a dark way, how to crave it.

"Remember you said that, Balthazar," she hissed at him.

It was meant as a dire warning, he was sure. Still, he took her chin in his hand and held her there, smiling hard when temper flooded her bright gaze.

"But one way or another, all this posturing or no, in the morning, you will be my wife," he told her, like an ancient omen. Like a curse. "And that will be an end to it."

CHAPTER NINE

KENDRA WASN'T THE sort of woman who had dedicated years of her life to fantasizing about her wedding one day. Not that there was anything wrong with such fantasies, but she'd always spent her time daydreaming about winning over her father's boardroom, and sitting behind suitably impressive desks in the family offices.

And she'd found herself fantasizing about far different things these days.

Still, if she'd thrown together a few wedding ideas off the top of her head, it would not have been...this.

It was a small affair on a particular stretch of the island that Panagiota informed her, with great seriousness, had been sanctified.

"Is that...good?" she asked.

"It is more than good," the other woman had replied. "It is necessary."

She'd woken the morning of her *sancti-fied* wedding her mouth feeling swollen and bruised from Balthazar's kiss the night before, though her inspection of her lips had indicated that sensation was rather more emotional than physical. Panagiota had come in, smiling merrily, her arms filled with a flowing white gown. Kendra was tempted to tear it up. Or demand something more suitable for the occasion, like a black shroud.

Maybe she would have done both of those things, but she made the mistake of running her hand over the filmy, flowy material of the gown when Panagiota carefully laid it out. And the next thing she knew, she was slipping it on.

Her body was changing, thickening by the day. She already had a significant belly. She was aware of her body in different ways these days. Clothes never quite fit the way she expected them to, and stranger still, her center of gravity had shifted.

But when she slipped the dress on, it was like a caress. It made her feel sensual and beautiful.

When she looked in the mirror, her heart constricted. Then it began to beat at her, hard.

Kendra told herself that she could make this forced wedding anything she wanted it to be.

She'd said a lot of things to Balthazar last night and then had stayed awake the rest of the night, wondering if any of them were true—because all he had to do was look at her and she trembled.

And after six weeks of solitude, she'd found she enjoyed that trembling. Maybe more than she should have.

"I want what I said to be true," she said out loud now as she stared at the vision in flowing white before her in the glass, her hand over her belly. Her baby grew by the day. Time was moving right along no matter what she said or didn't say to the man as caught in this as she was. "That will have to be enough."

She would make it enough.

Kendra did her own hair, bundling it up on the top of her head into a messy bun, then pinning it into place so it looked artistic rather than sloppy. She slicked on some lip gloss and decided against any blusher, as she could see she didn't need it. She didn't hide her freckles. She didn't bother to accentuate her eyes.

And strangely enough, she almost felt... free.

Because she knew that if one of those florid-cheeked boys her mother had forever been pushing on her was waiting for her today, her wedding would look nothing like this. She would have been sitting in her parents' house in Connecticut in a far more traditional gown, looking out at a huge tent on the lawn above the water. There would have been veils and churches and brigades of attendants. Guest lists filled with people she didn't know and didn't wish to know.

Maybe, Kendra thought, she'd never bothered to fantasize about her wedding day because it had always been a foregone conclusion. She certainly wouldn't have looked *happy* the way her reflection did.

Her heart did a cartwheel in her chest as she told herself, hurriedly, that was merely the pregnancy talking. The baby was giving her this glow. It wasn't *happiness.* It was hormones.

Either that, she thought when Panagiota came to collect her, or she'd taken leave of her senses entirely. Because as much as she might have shot her mouth off to Baltha-zar last night, she'd done what he wanted. She'd signed his agreements. She'd put on this dress.

For a woman who had claimed she had no intention of marrying him, Kendra was doing a terrific impression of a blushing, eager bride.

She waited for reality to slap her awake, but it didn't. Because this was reality. The baby inside her and the man waiting for her.

And both were better than anything involv-ing the life she'd left behind in Connecticut.

That was the truth that slapped her.

Hard.

Kendra tried to catch her breath from the wallop of it as the housekeeper led her through the sprawling villa, whitewashed walls and raucous flowers on all sides, then outside. Past all the terraces, past the ruins of a long-ago chapel, to a small altar on the side of a cliff.

There were three people waiting for her, seemingly suspended between the wide blue sky and the sun-drenched sea. Balthazar in his usual black, severe and unsmiling. The unfathomable priest. And another man she did not know, yet recognized instantly all the same.

Constantine Skalas, looking faintly rumpled and amused, as if he'd just that moment rolled off a supermodel and slouched his way to the ceremony.

As she drew closer, clutching the white gardenias Panagiota had handed her as they walked, Balthazar and the priest stared at her in varying degrees of condemnation. Constantine only smirked.

Kendra reminded herself that she was choosing to be as happy as she liked because she'd escaped the life her family wanted for her, which had to be worth a celebration, and beamed at all of them in turn.

"A white wedding," Balthazar murmured darkly as he took her arm. He did not *quite* scowl. "Let us hope God does not smite us down where we stand."

"This is the day our child becomes legitimate, Balthazar," she replied, smiling at him. Then more wildly when he actually did scowl at her. "Let us give thanks and be glad."

The ceremony was conducted in Greek and English. There were three rounds of blessings. Constantine exchanged their rings three times. There were candles and crowns, the joining of hands, and a ceremonial procession three times around the altar.

Kendra couldn't help being moved by the ancient words, the traditions, the press of Balthazar's hands against her own.

Like the baby inside her, *her* baby, the wedding felt bigger than her. It connected her to something far larger than herself or this man she was marrying or all the dark little squabbles that had brought them here.

Somehow, this wedding she hadn't wanted gave her hope.

She clung to that when it was over. Balthazar and his brother went off somewhere. Panagiota pressed a small bag of what she called *koufeta* into her hands—the word for sugared almonds, it seemed—then left with the priest.

Kendra spent her first moments as a married woman—as the wife of Balthazar Skalas—in a beautiful dress with gardenias and sugared almonds in her hands, alone at an altar. Unwilling to let go of that undeserved hope that ran through her as surely as the breeze.

She moved over to the railing and looked out at the deep blue Aegean Sea, because that felt like the same thing.

And she couldn't have said how long she stood there, but she was all too aware of it when Balthazar returned. She could *feel* him. That brooding, crackling energy, whipping all around her as if he brought his own storm with him wherever he went.

Kendra already knew he did.

"I'll admit it," she said, without looking over at him as he came to stand beside her, a dark and brooding cloud. "I expected to feel different."

"You should feel different. You are no longer a Connolly." He said that as if *Connolly* was a synonym for *rat*. The way he always did. "You are a Skalas."

"Oh, happy day."

They both stood there as the helicopter rose into the air from the pad on the other side of the villa, presumably taking Constantine and the unamused priest back to the mainland. Long after the sound of the propellers died away, they stayed there at the wedding altar.

Silent except for the beat of that same, familiar tension between them and the waves against the rocks below.

Until Kendra could take it no more and turned toward him, gazing up at the forbidding face of this man who was now her husband.

Her husband.

She had a heavy set of rings on her finger to prove it. More, she carried his baby inside of her—and felt the baby move, then. As if in agreement.

And Kendra tried to hold on to her sense of hope. To the beauty of the ceremony that had bound them together. She did. But she didn't understand how she could feel connected to this man in all these different ways, yet see no hint of that intimacy on his stern, remote face.

"What now?" she asked quietly. "Do the humiliations and punishments begin today? Or are we easing into them?"

"Such bravado. I wonder, would you retain it if I called your bluff?"

Kendra shrugged carelessly, though she did not feel careless in the least. Last night she had. Last night she'd felt powerful, because she'd grown comfortable here. The reality of this—of them—grew bigger within her all the time. *She* hadn't been hiding from it as he had.

She didn't know when that had changed. Was it the vows they'd spoken, in two languages? Had that made something shift inside of her?

"Go right ahead and call my bluff," she invited him. "But I intend to eat first. No one likes to be humiliated on an empty stomach."

She took her meal, still dressed in her full wedding regalia, on a different terrace with a different view of the enduring sea. *Teach me how to endure like that,* she thought, though she knew better than to say it aloud.

And then she applied herself to her wedding feast. There was a seafood salad of mussels and scallops, crab and calamari, all heaped together and marinated in lemon and the oil from the island's olives. There was a platter of tender lamb with tomato and orzo, topped with cheese. And when she was finished, heavenly baklava drenched in honey.

Kendra was not wholly surprised that Balthazar joined her, though he did not eat. Instead, he sat across from her. Brooding, clearly. She wondered if he meant to put her off her food, so she viewed it as a kind of rebellion that she ate her fill anyway.

Hope took many forms, she assured herself.

Then they both sat there, in more fraught silence, as their brand-new forced marriage entered its second hour.

"Well," she said after that went on for some time. "I will say that so far, I'm finding marriage a delight. But I didn't realize that we took a vow of silence. Was that the Greek part?"

A muscle in his jaw twitched. "We have yet to agree to terms."

"And here I thought I signed all kinds of papers last night. What was that, if not terms?"

"That was about money," Balthazar said in a certain, silken way. "But now you and I must decide the rest of it."

Her pulse picked up, kicking its way through her. And there was an answering surge of heat between her legs. But Kendra didn't want to show him her reaction, so all she did was lean back, smile, and wait.

"You have options, of course," he said, his dark eyes glittering and blocking out all the sun and sky. "But these choices have ramifications."

"Are we talking about consequences? Already?"

"I told you. I require a great deal of sex." And he said it so coldly. So devoid of passion that if she hadn't been looking directly at him she might have thought this was a clinical discussion. But she could see the way his eyes blazed. More, she could feel it, sharp and hot, in the softest part of her. Almost better than a touch. "Do you wish to provide it?"

"Why, Balthazar," she said softly. "Are you asking me to be your mistress as well as your wife? My cup runneth over."

It occurred to her to wonder as she said that, why, when he seemed to get grimmer by the moment, she was…moving in the opposite direction. Maybe it was because he'd married her. Maybe it was because she already loved, deeply, the child she carried—and somehow that splashed over on him, too.

Kendra shied away from that word. It came with deep, painful spikes.

All she knew was that she couldn't hate him the way she wanted to. God knew, she'd tried. She'd never quite gotten there, and now? She couldn't.

There had been crowns and rings and vows besides.

She *couldn't.*

"If you would prefer that this marriage remain in name only, I'm happy to oblige," Balthazar said with a certain dark inevitability. "I will find other means to meet my needs."

"An open marriage," Kendra said, nodding as if she discussed such things all the time. As if she didn't feel that strange hollow space yawn open inside of her. "I'm told many people in our tax bracket rely on these arrangements."

"We will not have an open marriage," Balthazar told her. It was a stern rebuke. "I do not share what is mine."

Her heart actually *hurt*, there beneath her too-tight ribs. But she made herself smile as if this was nothing more than idle talk over cocktails. "But you assume I do?"

"I told you that you have a choice. I do not recall telling you that you would enjoy the choice." He shrugged in that way of his, so supremely arrogant it should have left marks. "Either way, it is what it is."

Kendra opened her mouth to say something flippant, but something stopped her. Her breath caught in her throat, and she realized in the next second it was because he was holding himself so carefully. All of that leashed power, yes, but a certain glitter in those dark eyes made her wonder...

Something seemed to swell in her then. A kind of optimism, maybe. That same foolish hope.

If what you want is connection, intimacy, a voice in her said with a kind of calm practicality she associated with the great-aunt she'd hardly known, but who she felt she'd come to know over the months she'd spent living in that cottage, *you can't* fight *your way there. You can't demand vulnerability wearing battle armor and imagine it will come to you.*

And it was suddenly as if Kendra could see her whole life spinning around in front of her. As if it was contained in some kind of snow globe she held in her hands, already shaken hard. She'd wanted her father's attention. She'd wanted her brother's companionship. She'd wanted her mother's approval.

All of those were careful ways of saying she'd wanted their love.

That word with all its pain, its sharp edges and deep spikes.

She held her belly in her palms, and she

looked at this man who had wrecked her in a thousand ways already. That night on the gazebo. That night in his office. That kiss right here in this villa the night before. All that plus sacred vows and the sea as witness, and Kendra couldn't help thinking that, like it or not, she'd shown him more of herself than she had ever shown anyone else.

On the one hand, she thought maybe that was a sad thing, because she'd spent so long trying to shape herself according to other people's molds. But on the other hand, there was something about Balthazar—something so overwhelming and intense that she felt she could show him anything at all. That there was nothing she could reveal or do that would ruin it. He wasn't her father or brother, who would cut her off so easily if she didn't perform as they wished.

Oh, he said he was.

But she was sitting across from him now in a wedding dress. She wore his rings on her finger. Best of all, she could see the expression on his face.

And somehow, some way, she was sure she knew better.

Kendra didn't know much about sex. But she knew that this man had asked her to strip herself naked and she'd done it. She knew that this man had touched her and changed her forever. He'd moved inside her, and her life had no longer made any sense.

She'd changed it completely after that night, months before she would discover she was pregnant.

Maybe it was sex itself that was that powerful. But she didn't think so. Kendra had expected sex to be fun and maybe a little silly, because that was the way people spoke of it. That was what the movies showed her, dressing it up with a suggestive soundtrack and lighting it all up so it looked like art.

When instead, it was a haunting thing. It came to her still, woke her in the night, and infused her dreams with a dark, erotic need.

Not for sex.

For him.

And if Balthazar could have that kind of power, that meant she could, too.

She smiled, letting it widen as his eyes narrowed. That felt like a power all its own.

"I can't possibly make this choice with so little information," she told him. She waved a hand at him. Regally. "I will require an audition, of course. Isn't that how these things go?"

And then she nearly had to bite her tongue off to keep herself from laughing at the thunderstruck look of sheer, masculine astonishment on his arrogant face.

"I beg your pardon?"

"Don't be coy, Balthazar." She let out a laugh, then. She couldn't help it. "It's so unbecoming in a brand-new husband."

He bared his teeth at her. "I'm not following you."

"You are. You're just pretending not to." Kendra inclined her head at him. "Strip, please."

CHAPTER TEN

BALTHAZAR HAD NO intention of doing anything of the kind.

He gave the orders. He did not follow them.

But Kendra sat before him, a vision in flowing white and her hair pinned up to catch the kiss of the sun. Her cheeks were flushed, her freckles a tempting spray across her nose and over her bared shoulders. It made him want to do nothing but eat her like a dessert far sweeter than Panagiota's baklava.

Kendra was sugar and flame and all his now. His wife.

His *wife*.

Balthazar had not expected that word, common as it was, to get to him like this. Its meaning rocked through him, almost too hot to bear. He blamed that age-old ceremony and the words the old priest had spoken over them. He blamed the rings he'd slid onto her finger, the platinum catching the light and the diamonds so bright they nearly dimmed the sun.

But he could blame anything and everything. What he didn't understand was how she seemed to grow more beautiful by the moment, especially when this should have been a festival arranged around his revenge, not…whatever it was she imagined she was doing. He glared at her, but she only smiled, looking happy enough to wait forever for him to do as she'd demanded.

He could not imagine what made her imagine she had any power here.

Just as he could not imagine why he wasn't claiming his by right. And claiming her while he was at it.

"What's the matter?" she asked almost offhandedly, a gleam in those golden eyes of hers. "Don't tell me that the mighty Balthazar Skalas is afraid to do something here, on his own private island, that I did without blinking in the middle of a busy office? How funny. I thought you were meant to be the powerful one."

"Do you think goading me will work?"

She only smiled.

It turned that heat inside him…volcanic.

Before he knew it, Balthazar found himself rising from his seat. As he did, he took great pleasure in watching her eyes widen.

Not quite so sure of herself, then. No matter what she said.

And that made everything inside him run molten.

He made short work of his clothing. He shrugged out of the dark suit he'd worn for the ceremony, stripping down until he stood before her wholly naked. The sun poured all over him. The sea air was like a caress.

But best of all was that expression on Kendra's face.

It looked a great deal like *awe.*

He watched her flush. He watched that same giddy heat move its way down her neck. The dress she wore left her arms bare and he could see that same flush there, then goose bumps to match as she gazed up at him.

Balthazar felt everything shift. As if the world had spun about on its axis, then flattened him as it stopped still.

But he liked it.

Because he was the one standing naked before her, but he felt not a shred of supplication. No hint of weakness.

He had never felt more powerful in his life.

Had he called her names because he had sensed this, somehow? That a display of vulnerability led straight to something far more powerful? Had he wanted to diminish this very same light in her?

The notion sat uneasily in him. It pricked at him, reminding him of the reasons they were here, and married, and the revenge he had long ago vowed to rain down upon her father and the rest of her family...

But then he forgot it all. Because her eyes moved, almost convulsively, down over his chest. He was sure he could feel it like a touch over every ridge of his abdomen, every line of muscle. And she kept going until she found the hardest part of him, ready for her where he stood.

More than ready.

"If this is a proper audition," he managed to say, in a voice made harsh with need, "will you require the complete demonstration?"

When she lifted her gaze to his again, the wildfire he saw there made him want to roar like the beast he had always feared he was.

Though he didn't fear it now. Not when she looked at him as if the beast was precisely what she wanted.

God help him.

"Of course." Kendra's voice sounded husky now, though no less of a taunt. "Or how could I possibly make an informed decision?"

"How indeed."

Balthazar crossed to her then, bent down, and lifted her into his arms.

He spared no thought for his plans. The promises he'd made himself about how he would handle this marriage, how he would treat the wife he'd never wanted, how all of this would become part of what was owed Thomas Connolly. It all seemed inconsequential when he held her like this, her flowing dress wrapping around them as he moved, like tendrils of that same dream he always seemed to have when she was near.

He knew it wasn't true. It could never be true. And yet it haunted him.

Balthazar had intended to make it through his wedding secure in the purity of his fury. Secure in his hatred, his bitterness.

But when he'd looked up from the altar at the edge of the cliff to see Kendra coming toward him—in flowing white as she made her way through the ruins of the old chapel, flowers in hands and sunshine all over her face—the same dream that had woken him up in the night too many times to count now had walloped him all over again.

Constantine had murmured something that sounded suspiciously like *steady*.

Balthazar had been forced to ignore it, because the only other option was acknowledging that he had made some sound, or some face that allowed his brother to think he was ever anything but steady. That had proclaimed his weakness to the whole of the watching Aegean Sea.

And also because his bride was coming to him in the island breeze.

And for the time it took her to walk to his side, he tortured himself with fantasies of her innocence. He had never cared about such things before. It was only her. It was only this woman he could not bear to imagine with anyone else. Only this woman who he could not seem to imagine with anyone but him.

It should not have felt like torture, but she disturbed his sleep. The fantasy that she could come to him like that, bearing his child and no hand upon her but his… The dream that she might truly be his, without any bitterness coloring their days…

He knew better. He'd known better. Nothing had changed when he'd put a ring on her finger. No blessings, however sanctified, could change who they were.

And yet.

He carried her into the villa and took her straight to his private suite. It was a Greek daydream of archways to welcome in the sea and the sky. Everything was white and blue and then, there in the middle, his wife with her hair like flame and eyes of the brightest gold.

Like a treasure.

By the time he set her down gently at the foot of the wide, low bed, Balthazar was so hard, so greedy for her, that he was surprised she hadn't already burst into a thousand pieces with the force of it.

"Let me tell you how I want you to audition," she said, though she had to reach out to him to keep her balance and better still, she sounded breathless.

He found he liked that more than he should have. That no matter what—no matter the truth of things and the dark reality he would return to as soon as he did something about the hunger that was tearing him apart—he got to her, too.

"I find I have a particular take on the role," he told her, his voice dark. The greed in him like its own, beating pulse. "Why don't you tell me how you feel about it once I'm done."

This time, when he set his mouth to hers, he had no intention of stopping.

He kissed her, deep and long. He got his

hands in her hair, scattering the pins she'd used to secure it to the top of her head. It wasn't enough. No matter how he angled his head, no matter how close he held her, he wanted more.

He wanted everything.

Balthazar didn't understand this drive in him. This need. The dream and the greed, the *feelings* that battered at him, over and over, when he had been so certain for so long that he had none—

He felt as if something in him had broken. Yet as he held Kendra in his arms, he had the strangest notion that he had never been more whole.

That wasn't something he could take on board then, so Balthazar spun her around instead. He watched the deep, jarring breath she took as he worked to pull that dress up the length of her newly voluptuous body, then off.

Then she was before him in only a bra that wrapped around her back, holding her breasts as if on a shelf, and a skimpy pair of lace panties that made his mouth water. Her back was to him, so he indulged himself without worrying how his face might have been betraying him.

He put his mouth on the nape of her neck, then made his way down the tempting line of her spine. He removed that bra as he went, his hands trailing behind his mouth to graze her sides but not quite making it around to the particular temptation of those perfect breasts, now much larger than before. Not yet.

He found the small of her back and hooked his fingers in the lace he found high on her hips, then tugged it down as he bared the whole of her to his view.

Crouched there behind her, he turned her around so he could inhale the scent of her arousal. Sugar and heat. Then he indulged himself completely by licking his way directly into all of her soft, wet heat.

She jolted against him, making a shocked sort of sound that only made the greed in him worse. He was sure there was another lightning strike. He felt it go through her, and him.

Beneath his tongue, she quivered, but that was not enough. Not nearly enough.

Could anything be enough? something in him asked.

He wrapped one arm around her hips and pulled one of her legs over the width of his shoulder, opening her to him. Completely.

And then he devoured her.

She was sweet and he was savage. And the noises she made as she arched back, offering herself to him, pulsed in him like light. Like heat.

Like that greed he thought might never leave him.

He felt her convulse against his mouth, her body jerking as she sobbed out something incoherent that he thought might be his name.

And even as she shook, Balthazar was moving. He hauled her up into his arms again and then tumbled the both of them down into the embrace of that wide mattress.

She was still shaking, still making sobbing sounds, and for a moment he lost himself all over again in the slide of her flesh against his.

Skin to skin, head to toe, at last.

Balthazar felt as if he'd never had a woman before. As if he never would again. As if she was the beginning and the end of every-thing—and all he wanted to do was get closer.

Everything was heat and delight, a dark and encompassing glory.

All he wanted was that everything, even if it killed them both.

He rolled to his back and pulled her astride him. He watched, breathing hard already, as she braced herself against his chest, looking something like intoxicated when he knew she hadn't touched a drop of alcohol.

For that matter, neither had he—and that meant the spinning in his head was entirely due to Kendra.

He waited for her to shift herself into better position, to sheath him on a downward stroke he could almost feel already, but she didn't.

It was as if she was trying to focus on him. Her hair tumbled around her shoulders like another lick of flame. Balthazar wanted to taste each individual freckle he could see in that sweet spray across her nose, and more across her shoulders.

She was busy breathing, so he held her for a

moment. This woman who had come to him twice, both times at the bidding of men he despised. This woman he had taken from that cottage in France. This woman he had married and would call his wife, and who would be, no matter what else she was or became in time, the mother of his child.

For the first time, Balthazar let his gaze drop to her swollen belly, even more beautiful now that she wasn't wearing clothes to conceal it.

His heart beat at him in a new way, then. More intense. More wild and dangerous.

A different kind of greed.

Balthazar slid his hands over her belly. He heard her breath catch, and though he ordered himself not to do it, he looked up and caught her gaze.

And for a moment he forgot who they were.

For moment he was nothing more and nothing less than a man holding the pregnant belly of a woman, both of them fully aware that the child they'd made was just there, just inside.

She sat astride him and a different kind of electricity moved between them. He could feel it. It was part of him, part of her. Not a lightning strike from elsewhere, but made from this. From the heat they sparked between them, and had from the moment she'd stepped into that gazebo.

He was unsurprised and something like furious and deeply glad all at once when she moved her hands to cover his.

And for a long while there was only breath. There was only this.

Only *this*.

There was creation and revelation. Wonder and hope. Sex and need and a baby woven into the middle of that.

Woven so tightly it only then occurred to Balthazar that he'd been kidding himself all this time to imagine that this wasn't the very point of…everything.

This was life. Kendra had brought him *life*.

And in that moment, Balthazar could not bring himself to care what her reasons might have been. What her agenda was, then or now.

In that moment, he forgave her anything and everything, because there was this. The two of them, skin to skin. Their hands tangled up together to hold the new life they'd created.

The two of them breathing new life into him. Into her.

There was a *them.*

A family, something in him whispered.

It hit him like an explosion. A burst of near-incapacitating sensation.

It burned him alive.

"I need you," Balthazar gritted out. "Now."

And for a moment, he could have sworn that she was baffled. She blinked at him as if the words he used made no sense.

He shifted his hands to her hips, to grip her and move her into place. As he shifted her it seemed to dawn on her what she could do. She blew out a breath, then leaned forward, bracing herself on his chest.

Then he watched, somehow thrown and charmed at once, as she awkwardly tried to lift herself to take him within her.

And failed.

"Surely we are past this now," he said, his voice gravelly with need. He reached between them to grab his own length and guide himself to her softness. God help him, to her *heat*. It nearly undid him. "I have already married you, Kendra. What is the point of continuing to play these games?"

"What games?" she asked, panting a bit as she wriggled against him, as if attempting to slot him into place.

As if she'd never done something like this before.

But that was not possible.

"I do not require you to pretend to be innocent," he managed to say as she was poised there above him, her hair falling down to cocoon the both of them in all that fire.

His dreams could go to hell. This was better.

"Of course I'm not innocent," Kendra replied with a laugh, holding herself up with her thighs splayed wide. "You took care of that in New York."

"What does that mean?"

She blew out another breath as if gearing herself up. Then she took him into her body with a sudden thrust, sheathing him fully.

Finally.

Sensation punched through him. He almost lost his control, but wrenched back, barely.

Barely.

And she couldn't have meant what he thought she'd meant. He was half-mad with wanting her, that was all.

"What do you mean about New York, Kendra?" he demanded, ordering himself to wait. To hold on.

To hear her answer before he lost his head.

"Oh," Kendra said, sounding flustered and breathless. Sure enough, that telltale flush rolled down the length of her body, lighting her up as surely as a billboard in Times Square. "I thought you knew already. I was a virgin that night."

And then she began to move.

CHAPTER ELEVEN

HER BODY WAS different now. Kendra felt awkward in her clothes and sometimes couldn't figure out how to move the way she'd used to. There were new aches and strange pains in all kinds of surprising places, but this—

This was the same.

Better.

Balthazar was deep inside her again. At last. And this time, she was fully aware of every inch of his flesh and the fact that there was nothing between them.

This time, there was no pain.

There was only the reality of him, hard and thick, filling her so completely that it was almost too much. Almost. She had to keep moving so that the sensation grew, but never quite tipped over into pain again.

The more she moved, the better it felt.

And there was something about the look on his face as he gazed up at her. An intensity so close to a scowl that if she'd been doing anything else, she might have frozen in place—

But there wasn't a single part of her that wanted to stay still. Much less freeze.

Instead, she braced herself against him, leaned into all that glorious heat, and let her hips do as they wished.

She took him inside her, then lifted herself away. She was fully aware of the moment he took over that rhythm, moving her instead of letting her rock herself against him, and that was better.

Everything he did was better.

Sitting up like this, different sensations buffeted her with every thrust. Her breasts bounced gently. There was a stretch in her thighs that seemed to arrow straight to the place they were joined. And that new belly of hers changed how she fit against him.

Or maybe it was as simple as the position. How would she know?

Balthazar muttered something she didn't understand, a rough scrape of Greek. Then he tugged her lower so he could take one of her nipples deep into his mouth.

And just like that, shockingly *quickly*, Kendra shattered all over again.

But he didn't stop. He took his time with her oversensitive breasts and she kept falling apart. Again and again.

He switched his attention from one breast to the other, his hand taking over when his mouth abandoned the job. Back and forth, back and forth, and all the while he maintained that steady, even pounding rhythm deep inside her.

At first Kendra counted the times he made her dissolve.

Three times. Four.

Then she lost count. There were too many flames, setting her alight, making her scream. Making her forget there was anything but this.

But him.

Then Balthazar was rolling her over and stretching her out below him as he propped himself up on his arms. And suddenly he was even deeper, so much a part of her that she thought she could die like this, connected in ways she had never known were possible—

He was saying Greek words as he gazed down at her, as hot as his mouth against her pulse. And he lost that steady rhythm, pounding into her as he took her to that edge once more.

And this time when she bucked against him, fragments of her flying all around and shattering so completely she was sure she would never put herself back together again, he came with her.

For a long, long while, Kendra thought maybe they had died, after all. There was no other explanation for how she felt, floating and perfect and beautiful. Or the rawness of her despair when he moved, withdrawing from her body and rolling over to his back.

It took her some time to realize that her heart was still beating like a drum, but her breath was starting to even out.

And that he had moved to sit with his back to her, there on the edge of the wide bed.

Kendra thought she ought to do something about that, but found when she tried that she lacked the strength. Her whole body appeared to be made of wet clay.

"I will need you to explain yourself," Balthazar said, his voice grim. "Now."

It was a lot like a bucket of ice water in the face, if she was honest.

But even that felt like a pageant of sensation, mixed in with all the rest, so all Kendra did was turn over to her side. She propped herself up on her elbow and wished, with a passionate sort of fervency that might have alarmed her in any other circumstances, that she dared reach out and trace her fingers over the proud line of his strong back.

She hated that she did not dare. That she had married him, was having his baby, and had discovered that they could do these marvelous things to each other...but she did not quite dare a touch.

But he had married her. He had promised her many things at that altar above the sea, but he had not told her it would be easy. "What must I explain?"

Balthazar did not look at her, and still she could sense his scowl. She could feel it. He wasn't the thundercloud, Kendra realized. He was the storm.

And what did it say about her that she wanted nothing more than to dance in it?

She saw him tense. "You came to my office. Your bargaining chip was your body. You stripped down immediately… There's no possible way you could have been innocent that night. None."

"If you say so."

He turned then, twisting around so that she could see a kind of anguish in his face. And worse, a different, searing condemnation in his thunderclap gaze. "You had already tried the game once before, in that gazebo. We both knew the truth of it."

"In the gazebo?" Kendra's heart beat as if she ought to be upset by this, but she was still having trouble following what was happening. How could he be so grim and growly when she wanted nothing more than to start all over again? "I had no idea you were there. I was trying to take a breather in the middle of one of my parents' tedious parties, that was all. And then you were there and your mouth was on me, and I didn't know what to do."

"No. *No.* This is impossible."

A laugh escaped before she could stop it. "Would you prefer that I was the tramp you've always thought I was?"

But then something in her turned over. Because she recognized the expression that moved over his face. He did wish that.

And in the next moment, she understood.

"I thought this was simply how you treat women," she breathed.

Suddenly Kendra felt exposed. Ugly. She sat up and looked around in a bit of a panic for something to cover herself with, but there was only the frothy heap of her wedding gown at the foot of the bed. She pulled it to her, holding it against her like a shield.

Waiting, she knew, for him to say something. To deny it.

But he didn't.

"This isn't how you treat *most women*, is it?" she asked softly, though she wanted to scream. "This is how you treat me. It's not that you think women are whores. It's that you think *I* am. That I always have been."

"Why would your father or your brother send me a virgin sacrifice?" Balthazar thundered. "Don't they know—"

But he cut himself off. Kendra pulled the dress tighter against her chest.

"And, of course, a whore deserves to be stripped naked and humiliated," she said quietly, because she understood too many things now. His fury. His coldness. He'd used the word—maybe it was her fault for thinking he didn't mean it. Maybe if she'd had more experience, she would have. "Dispatched by her equally repellent family to do their calculated work, she deserves zero consideration. A quick tumble on a desktop and nothing but cruel words. What I don't understand is why, if that is what you think of me, you didn't wrap your entire body in latex to avoid the situation we find ourselves in now. To say nothing of other…contaminants."

"I lost my head," he growled at her. "I could not understand why I kept imagining your innocence when it was so plainly long gone. Now I know."

And she could have sworn that sounded like…grief.

"Which is it, husband?" she asked. "Are you angry that I'm not as free with my favors as you thought I was? Are you angry that I didn't tell you when I think we both know you wouldn't have believed me? Or is it the uncomfortable notion that if I'm not who you thought I was…neither are you?"

"Is this the true game?" he demanded. "Is this what you've wanted all along, Kendra? To tie me in knots, crowd my head, make me into a madman? What does your father think will be gained by this kind of deception?"

She blinked at that, still holding the dress close. "My father? What does my father have to do with this?"

"Did he not send you to me in the first place?"

"He didn't send me to the gazebo. He did send me to New York. What he did not do, ever, was even so much as hint that he was interested in whether or not I was in possession of my virginity."

The very idea of discussing virginity with her father made her stomach turn.

Balthazar looked as if he might reach for her then, and Kendra wanted that so much she could feel moisture collect in the corners of her eyes.

But instead he pushed himself off the bed and moved across the bedroom. He stopped in one of the grand archways that opened over a graceful terrace and stood there, staring out toward the sea.

The sun poured in, making him seem like some kind of stone carving, polished to shine. Not a man at all.

Because he was no longer looking at her, she indulged herself and pressed the heel of her hand against the place where her heart beat so hard it hurt.

"You should have told me," he said a long while later, his voice thick. Dark.

"What would have been the point?" she asked simply.

Even from across the room, she could hear

the way he drew in a breath at that, and it made her heart hurt even more.

Kendra gathered the dress around her, like a security blanket. She remembered how she'd felt earlier, walking to him where he stood on the edge of that cliff.

As if together they might fly off into all that blue and stay there, as limitless as the horizon.

"Balthazar," she said softly now. "What if we made a different kind of bargain altogether?"

The hand he'd propped up against the side of the open arch clenched into a fist.

Kendra decided to take that as encouragement. Or as a sign, anyway, that she was on the right track. Since he could so easily have shot her down already.

She slid one hand to her belly. She thought about her father and brother, even her mother, and the lives they'd all chosen. Then she thought about Great-Aunt Rosemary, who had walked away from that very same life and done as she pleased.

We can make our lives whatever we wish

them to be, her great-aunt had written in loopy cursive on the first page of one of the journals she'd left for Kendra to read.

Kendra could start right now.

"What if we removed everybody else from the table?" she asked softly. "What if all we thought about was you and me and our child? You're going to be a father, Balthazar. I'm going to be a mother. We'll both be the parents of this baby, and that means something. To the baby, I have to think it will mean the world."

The words were pouring from her mouth, though she couldn't have said where they were coming from. They seem to be connected to the blood that pumped through her veins. The soft, hot core of her that was already hungry for him again. The heaviness in her breasts. And the rounded belly he had caressed so gently, making her feel like a fertility goddess. More beautiful than she'd ever been.

She had taken so few chances in her life. She had dared so little—except when it came to him.

But she thought of the crowns they'd worn today and the rings on their hands. She thought of that look of wonder on his face when he'd gazed up at her, both of them holding tight to the future they'd made.

It had to mean something. She would *make it* mean something.

She took a breath. "What if we decided, you and me, to be a family?"

He turned back to her then, though he didn't come closer. He stood there with the light all around him and his gaze bleak.

Kendra fought off a shiver.

"Families like yours?" he asked with a certain, quiet menace. "An overly medicated mother. A morally corrupt father, who would prostitute his virgin daughter to protect his son from the consequences of his own deceitful actions. A man who knows no boundaries, who respects no limitations, who always and ever does only what pleases. What an enticing prospect."

Kendra would have listed any number of reasons she was not thrilled with her family at the moment, but she didn't like him doing it. "Families are complicated. Yours certainly is—you told me so yourself."

He moved toward her then, something terrible on his face.

It didn't make him any less beautiful.

"And would you like to know *why* my family is as complicated as it is?" he asked, his voice stark.

Kendra admitted to herself that in that moment, she really didn't.

"When my mother came back from her stay in her private hospital, she tried to make amends. With my brother and me, it was easy. We loved her." Balthazar's eyes had gone cold. "With my father, on the other hand, she had much less success."

"The poor woman," Kendra breathed.

"My father hated my mother for her weakness," Balthazar told her. "Whether that was just or not is beside the point. It happened. After a while, I found myself following suit." Kendra let out a ragged sort of sound, but that only made his mouth curve into something grim. "He beat me into his image, Kendra. Constantine was permitted his little rebellions but I never was. It was easy to take everything my father said as gospel. My mother was weak. She deserved no loyalty from my father. He believed this and so did I. He acted it out and so did I. *I believed it.*"

"Beliefs do not live in your bones, they live in your head and your heart," Kendra threw right back at him. "They're not facts, Balthazar. They're feelings. You can change them. All you have to do is want to."

"If only it were that simple."

"What in life is simple?" She found herself moving to her knees, still clasping the wedding gown before her, like an offering now. "Do you think that I wanted to find myself pregnant with the child of a man who made it clear he hated me?"

"Yes," he said, the simple syllable cutting deep into her. "Until today I assumed that was exactly what you wanted."

Kendra was terrified she might break down into tears. And she couldn't bear it. She crawled over to the edge of the bed and stood, pulling the dress up and over her head once more.

And the irony wasn't lost on her that she stood there, wedded and bedded and discarded at dizzying speed. Barefoot and pregnant. A collection of worst nightmares, really.

She almost thought she should laugh at the absurdity. But the laughter wouldn't quite come.

"You really thought I got pregnant on purpose?"

The look on his face made her hug herself. "My father believed in consequences," Balthazar told her in that same grim tone. "When I was a small boy, he beat me himself. As I grew older and bigger, he used other means of punishment. Sometimes he would beat my brother for my infractions. Other times, he would do things he knew hurt my mother. In time, he promised me, I would stop caring about either, and he was right."

"He sounds like a broken, horrible man, and what does that have to do with us? Or this baby?"

"He raised me to care about the business alone, as he did," Balthazar continued, as if he had no choice. As if these things were being dragged out of him whether he liked it or not. "And I thought it made sense that he should have his other women if he wished, because he was the one who worked so hard to build the Skalas empire. What did my mother do but waft around the house, haggard and pathetic?"

His voice was hard, like bullets, but somehow Kendra thought he was aiming the gun at himself.

"A friend of his started to spend more time with the family," Balthazar continued, a stark, ferocious thing on his face. He stood there, much too still, and though all Kendra wanted to do was go to him, she knew better. She knew he wouldn't allow it. "He flattered my father. He took an interest in what Constantine and I were doing. And then, because he could, he started an affair with my mother. Right under my father's nose."

"But your father was already having his own affairs, wasn't he?"

Balthazar shrugged. "He was not a rational man when it came to the things he considered his. When my father discovered this affair, he confronted the two of them. He made my brother and me witness it, because he said it affected the family. I was sixteen."

"Balthazar…" she whispered.

"My mother was regretful, but she said they were in love. That he was kind to her, which was more than my father had been. That she would sign whatever he liked if he let her go." His grim expression did not alter in the slightest. "But his friend only laughed. He called my mother names and told my father it was no more than he deserved for some or other business deal. He left my mother sobbing on the floor."

"You shouldn't have seen that," Kendra said fiercely. "Your father should have protected you from that."

"He was too busy throwing my mother out," Balthazar said icily. "And when she went, she fell apart."

He ran a hand over his face, then. Maybe she only thought she saw it shake.

"You don't have to tell me the rest of this," she said, even as she racked her brain to remember what had become of his mother. Why did she think it was something sad?

"But I do," he replied. He started toward her then, slow and deliberate. "My mother descended into a squalid little life of men who took advantage of her. She turned to drink. Then to drugs. One night she took too much and slipped into a coma. She has never awoken. She lies there still, slowly wasting away, trapped in her despair."

Kendra's pulse rocketed around inside her. Her stomach twisted. But still he drew closer in that same, terrible way. She wanted to run, but she wanted to stay where she was even more. As if she was proving something.

"My brother and I vowed that we would take our revenge on the man who targeted her," Balthazar said, the ring of something heavy in his voice. And stamped all over his face. If she didn't know better, knowing this man as she did, she might have imagined it was guilt. "No matter how long it took. No matter what it entailed."

"Do you mean your father?"

His smile was thin. "My father did not help,

I grant you. But it was not he who pushed my mother over the side of that cliff. It was not he who used her, then discarded her, and laughed about what he'd done."

"You said he was unkind to her."

"He was unkind," Balthazar snapped. "Had she never met this friend of his, she would have survived it like the rest of us."

"I don't blame you for hating him," Kendra said softly.

Balthazar's eyes blazed. He stopped moving, though he was still more than an arm's length away from her.

"I am delighted to hear you say that, Kendra," he said. "Because the man I am speaking of is your father."

It was like the world dimmed, or she slid off the side of it. She stared back at him, convinced her ears were ringing. Convinced her heart had stopped. Convinced she must have misheard him.

But none of those things were true.

"Your father," he said again, so there could be no mistake, "drove my mother to her current state. And has never looked back. He prefers to dance around me in business situations as if I don't know what he did. What he is."

"But…. But you…"

"I assumed you were nothing but another knife he thought to plunge in the side of my family," Balthazar said. "Some men deal with their guilt in extravagant ways. Of course he sent you to me. I have no doubt his greatest hope was that history would repeat itself."

"All along," Kendra whispered. "All along you've…" She felt as if she might collapse, but she didn't. "You don't just hate me, do you, Balthazar? You want to use me to hurt him. You didn't take your revenge—you made me become it."

He bared his teeth as if the pain was too great. As if the villa they stood in was nothing but ash and ruins at their feet.

But she couldn't tell if he wanted it that way, and it broke her heart.

"And I might have dreamed of your innocence, Kendra," he managed to grit out, turned once again to a storm. She could feel the rain on her face. She could hear the thunder in his voice. "I might have imagined what it would be like if you are not as tarnished as the people you come from. But that is not who we are. And this marriage is nothing more than a weapon I will use to cut down a monster."

"Balthazar…" she whispered, agonized. "You can't mean that. You can't."

His mouth was a merciless lash. "You should have run when you had a chance, Kendra. I regret that you are not the woman I thought you were. But you will pay all the same."

And then he left her there, in her wedding gown with his scent all over her like a curse, to let her tears fall at last.

Alone.

CHAPTER TWELVE

BALTHAZAR MEANT TO leave the island entirely.

He stormed from the bedchamber and pulled on the first clothing he could find in the attached dressing room. He would go to Athens, he decided. He would do what he had always done and lose himself in work. In the business. In the things that made him who he was and more, who he wished to remain.

The things that mattered, he thought.

And thinking of what mattered, perhaps heading back to New York made even more sense. He headed for the office suite he kept in the villa, finding all of his devices charged and ready for him, but he didn't pick up his mobile. He didn't give the order to have the helicopter readied for the flight to the mainland. Instead, he found himself staring at the desk before him, seeing nothing.

Nothing but the choices that had brought him here.

And wrapped around everything, shot through it all, he saw Kendra's face. Her beautiful face and her lovely eyes filled with tears.

Tears he had put there, Balthazar knew.

He saw the way she'd stared at him, clutching that dress to her chest as if he was nothing more than a rampaging beast. A soulless monster, as he'd often been accused.

As if he'd finally become his father.

All the way through, at last.

Balthazar pushed away from the desk, moving without thought, almost as if he was trying to get away from that realization when it should have been cause for celebration. He should have been thrilled that he'd finally achieved what had long been the goal of his entire existence on this earth.

Demetrius Skalas had prided himself on his single-minded, emotionless pursuit of the bottom line. He had eradicated weakness, he had claimed. He felt nothing and took pride in it. He acted only in the interests of the company. Even the succession of beautiful women he sported on his arm, each one a blow to his despised wife, Demetrius claimed elevated his profile in the eyes of the world—and more importantly, in the eyes of the other titans of industry he considered his peers. All of whom preferred to do business with men they admired.

They had all admired Demetrius.

Balthazar had taken his beatings as a child, and had come to believe that his father was right—they made him stronger. And as he grew, he had dedicated himself, in word and deed, to following his father's example. To locating and removing every hint of weakness he could find.

In place of any stray emotions, he had tended his thirst for revenge.

And in place of the pesky feelings that plagued other men, he had plotted the downfall of Thomas Connolly and his pathetic son.

Then she had come along and turned everything on its ear.

He found himself outside, the island drenched

in the beauty of the setting sun, though all he saw was the past.

A past that was threaded through with the same driving goal, always. Balthazar had told himself that he was giving Tommy Connolly rope to hang himself with while, over the course of years, he'd sat back and watched his enemy's son steal from him. In the months since Kendra had given herself to him in New York, he had continued to wait.

Now, standing outside as the breeze picked up as the sun made its lazy descent, he had to question that choice.

He had told himself it was because he was waiting. To see if Kendra was with child. To see if it was time to flip the script on his revenge and approach it a different way—one that would involve his in-laws. Surely that required a different tack, he'd assured himself. He'd felt perfectly prepared to handle whatever came of Kendra's potential pregnancy. First and foremost, he'd been thinking of the child's legitimacy and the wedding he'd never imagined for himself.

What he hadn't thought to reckon with were emotions.

Balthazar had congratulated himself on feeling nothing for Kendra—because surely, his abiding, distracting hunger for her didn't count. Surely his obsession with her, with what she was doing and where she was going and every expression that crossed her pretty face, was about that same physical hunger.

It was nothing more, he'd told himself, time and again. Nothing but sex, lust and need.

He might not have liked those things in him, making him as basic as any other man, but they were understandable.

What he had not been prepared for was her pregnancy. Not the fact of it, which he'd seen coming or he wouldn't have tracked her. But that wave of emotion that had struck him earlier. It had felt something like sacred when, together, they had held their hands over her belly and the life that grew within.

How could he possibly have prepared for that?

But even as he asked himself that question, he knew that there was another, more pointed query he needed to make. Just as he knew everything in him wanted to avoid it.

He walked until he reached the edge of one of the cliffs, then stood there, bracing himself. His hands were in fists at his side while the sun seemed to pause in its fall toward the sea to hit him full in the face.

A bit too much like clarity for his tastes.

And all he could see was the golden shimmer of Kendra's eyes, as if she was here before him, watching him.

Waiting for him, something in him whispered.

"Beliefs do not live in your bones, they live in your head and your heart," she had told him. *"You can change your feelings, Balthazar. All you have to do is* want *to."*

He had never wanted to do anything of the kind. He had never wanted to feel a thing.

And now he felt ravaged by these *feelings*.

Enemies he could fight. He was good at that. It only took waiting, watching, and then striking their weaknesses when they presented themselves.

But how could he fight this?

Kendra had used the word *family*. That damned word.

Worse, she had suggested that the two of them could make their own, and he had seen the hope in her gaze when she'd said it.

God help him, but he had no defense against *hope*.

He wanted to reject it the way he had rejected her. He wanted to already be far away from here, winging his way back to the only life he knew.

But he couldn't make himself turn around. He couldn't make himself leave.

Because her hope was infectious.

And if he accepted that, he accepted that he was far, far weaker than he'd ever imagined.

Because he'd dreamed all of this, hadn't he? Balthazar had tortured himself, not simply with fantasies of availing himself of her beautiful body and slaking that hunger for her that had haunted him across the years. But more, he'd dreamed of her innocence. And not because he had ever put any great stock in virginity, as it was simply one more thing men liked to use for barter, whether women wished it or not.

But because innocence felt like a shortcut to a different life.

He thought of his poor mother, wrecked so many years ago. Long before she'd been tossed out by his father, she'd been left to fend for herself while Demetrius had cheated on her. After they'd divorced, Demetrius had repeated his behavior with any number of subsequent wives—but none of *them* could claim they hadn't known what they were getting into.

His first wife, the mother of his sons, had been blindsided. And what had been the sin that Demetrius had believed *deserved* the way he'd responded? Balthazar had stopped asking himself that when he was still a boy.

But he knew the answer now.

His mother had felt far too much and Demetrius had despised her for it.

Balthazar had learned to do the same.

He looked down at his hands, uncurling his fingers so he could see the flat of his palms.

He could still feel the warmth of Kendra's

belly, the life she carried within. And then, finally, asked himself the question he'd been avoiding since the night he'd realized that he'd had sex with Kendra Connolly without using any protection.

Did he truly wish to do to his child what his father had done to him?

He thought about taking his own hands, the ones he gazed at there on that cliffside, and raising them against his own child. He thought of carrying out this second phase of his revenge as he'd planned when the child was no more than a possibility instead of a fact, taking it to its logical extreme.

Did he plan to make *his baby* hate its mother?

Was that who he was?

His heart kicked at him, too hard and too loud. And Balthazar tried to tell himself that there was no other way. That he had committed himself to this path and that was the end of it. But the dreams he'd had told him differently.

So had Kendra.

And if Balthazar could decide to be any

man he chose, there was only one real question left. Would he choose to be this one?

Because suddenly, as the sun painted the sky the bright, brilliant shades of gold that reminded him only of Kendra, he looked back and saw the life he'd been living in a very different light than he would have if he'd considered it six months ago.

He had become his father after all. Cold. Unfeeling. Half monster, half machine, and proud of the worst parts of both. Dedicated entirely to a business that already had made him more money than he could ever spend in his own lifetime. Or ten successive lifetimes.

As if that mattered.

It seemed to him here, now, that it was stark. Empty.

A lifeless existence.

Until Kendra had come in and infused the prison he hadn't even realized he lived in with all of her bright color.

How could he sentence his child to that same cell?

And it took him a moment to realize that what walloped him then was grief.

For the mother he had lost when he was young, then had pushed away when she returned because he'd thought that might please his father. Only accepting the guilt and shame he'd felt over her treatment when it was too late for her. No amount of revenge in her name was ever going to change the fact that he was the one who had abandoned her.

And another kind of grief seized him, because while he had seen his father for who he was, Balthazar had always imagined himself immune. He'd been expected to be immune. He'd known Demetrius was a cruel man, certainly. A viciously cold one. A father who could not love and refused to allow such soft sentiments in anyone near him. A man who had raised two sons with enough violence that they felt that they dared not attempt it themselves.

Balthazar could do the same, of course. That had been his plan.

But for the first time he understood, not only how much damage had been done to him, but what he had lost.

How much he had lost.

That he had such darkness in him made him despair of himself. But the greater punch of grief was that, had it not been for Kendra and this baby he would have sworn he did not want, he might never have seen the truth about himself so clearly.

If it weren't for Kendra, he would never have known.

He tried to fight it, but it was no use. Night was coming, bringing with it the heartless stars, each and every one of which seemed to punch their way inside of him.

And he could call it what he liked.

But Balthazar understood that the emotion he'd been avoiding the whole of his life had come for him, at last.

And it was no mystery to him why his father had abhorred them so. Emotions were messy. They tore through him now, storm after storm, never ceasing and always changing, making a mockery of the anger he tried to throw up as a shield.

He took it, one hurricane after the next turning him inside out and then slapping him back together as if he could ever be the same.

When he knew better. Because he'd seen colors now, and there was no way to go back from that. There was no way to make himself willfully blind.

Even if he had tried, he knew that he didn't have it in him to sentence his child to that same stark and lifeless fate.

He was Balthazar Skalas. He surrendered to no man.

Lucky for him, then, that the only person on earth he intended to surrender to was a woman. His wife.

Assuming she would have him now that she knew the truth about her family and his, and the great, ugly weight of the revenge he'd tried so hard to take out on her.

He turned, surprised to find that he'd made his way to the altar where he had married her a lifetime ago on this very same, endless day. The ruins of the old chapel gleamed in the starlight and for moment, when he saw movement, he thought it was an apparition.

Or better still, that dream of his, come to comfort him once more.

But as she moved closer, he saw that it really was Kendra.

His heart skipped a beat.

She still wore her wedding gown, that flowing, frothy gown that gleamed an unearthly white in the starlight. And she looked wilder than she had this morning, as if the daylight had required compliance, but here in the dark, there was only her.

Her hair was a tousled flame, and he longed to run his hands through it all over again. He could see traces of the tears she'd cried, there on her cheeks as she drew closer, but she was not weeping now. If anything, she looked determined.

His own little warrior, who could not stop fighting, no matter what.

Balthazar had a vision of her in his New York office so long ago and felt his heart lurch all over again. In those moments before she'd seen him she'd stood at the window, staring out at the glittering sprawl of Manhattan. Her face had been so soft, suffused with that sweet heat that had entranced him, even then.

He had told himself he was unmoved, but that had been a lie.

And he'd waited longer than he should have, drinking her in. Something he would have denied to the death if she'd called him on it.

Something he couldn't have admitted then, especially to himself.

Kendra stopped before him, the breeze making her seem half ghost, though he knew better. She was made of warmth and sunlight, even in the dark.

Maybe especially in the dark.

"I was sure that you would be halfway to New York by now," she said.

There was a roaring thing in him, but he ignored it. "I intended to be."

"And yet here you are."

"Here I am," he agreed.

And it felt...portentous. Huge. The roaring in him and that white gown in the breeze and the stars all around them, as if they knew.

Her gaze searched his. Balthazar wished that he could understand what he saw there. And he wished even more that he could find the words to tell her what had happened to him. *In* him. What she'd done to him.

But it all seemed inadequate when there was Kendra, staring up at him with that same openness as if he had not hurt her. Again and again.

"You should run from me, little one," he said then. "Screaming, and in the opposite direction."

"What would be the point of that?" she asked. Her lips curved. "This is a very small island. And I have no interest in drowning myself."

He frowned at that, and that hint of levity when he wished to take responsibility, at last, for who and what he had become—

Kendra swayed closer to him, placing her hands on his chest.

And Balthazar…was unarmed.

He stared down at her hands, one of them bedecked in the rings he'd put there this morning. As he did, he became vaguely aware that he'd thrown on trousers and a haphazardly buttoned shirt, so that both of them were in white.

As if that made up for anything.

But it was her touch that astonished him. That would have broken him, he thought, had there been anything in him left to break.

"I told you that I'm your enemy," he said then, his voice severe. "Since the moment I knew who you were, I have thought of nothing but crushing you, Kendra. You must know this."

"I know it." And though her lips were still curved, there was a certain steel in those golden eyes of hers. "But you are also my husband. And the father of my child. And I do not choose to be crushed, Balthazar."

"Is it your choice?" he asked, though even as he did, he found himself moving to trap her hands there against his chest. To hold her, despite himself.

When he knew he should not tempt himself. That he did not deserve it. Or her.

"I want to be outraged, but I'm not," she told him, almost solemnly. "I want to defend my father's behavior, but I can't. I tried to come up with excuses, but I don't have any. The truth of the matter is that I'm not surprised to hear what he did to your mother. To you. Disappointed, maybe. But not, I'm afraid, surprised."

"Do not forgive me, Kendra," Balthazar gritted out. "Not so easily. You have no idea the kind of darkness that lives in me."

"But I do know it," she replied, to his astonishment. And that gaze of hers was steady on him, the sun to the earth. "I know your darkness, Balthazar. I know your fury, your retaliation. I know your absence and I know your touch. And I can tell you, with every part of my soul, that there is nothing you can do that would make me abandon you. Or I would already be swimming for the mainland."

All the broken parts of him seemed to vibrate with the same ferocity, then. And still all he could see was her gaze, as if the sun had not yet set. As if she lit up the world.

She did it effortlessly.

"I don't know how to do anything but plot revenge," he threw at her. "I could stand here and tell you all the things I think I feel, but how would I know? Feelings were my first enemy and I vanquished them long ago. You deserve more than a broken man."

"I deserve you," she countered. Then she leaned in, to underscore the intensity on her face. "Because you have haunted me, Balthazar, since the moment I looked up and found you in that gazebo. My brother and my father might have had their own reasons for sending me to see you in New York, but I didn't have to go. I wanted to. I wanted to see you. And let's be very clear. I wanted to strip for you. I wanted your touch. I wanted everything that's happened between us, because if I hadn't, I could have walked away at any time."

He wanted to believe that. Which was why he couldn't. "I kidnapped you, Kendra. You can't handwave that away."

"I'm not the hapless maiden sent off to sacrifice herself to the village dragon, despite appearances," Kendra said, with laughter in her voice. Actual laughter. "I could have ducked away from you when we went to your doctor in Athens. Failing that, Panagiota might have restricted access to the internet here but if I'd really, truly wanted to get online I could have found a way. I didn't want to."

"Kendra…" He managed to breathe. Barely. "Kendra, I can't…"

The stars were upon them and around them, the sea whispered their names, and Balthazar felt caught somewhere between that light from up above and all the sunlight in her gaze. As if all that brightness could make of him a better man.

"I want to promise you that I will change," he told her, though his heart hurt and he wanted things he could hardly identify. But that wanting never eased, not where she was concerned. Maybe it never would. "But I can only hope I will. I want to promise you the world, the stars above us now and the ground beneath our feet. I want to promise you that I will learn to be the kind of man who can love, and hope, and raise our child with those things instead of the back of my hand or the sting in my words. I have done a great many things in this life, Kendra. I was given a fortune and I made five more. I have feared no man I've ever met. I have faced every challenge set to me. All this, yet I have never loved. I…"

He wasn't sure he could continue. But her eyes had gone bright again, gleaming with emotion.

All that emotion, like color, changing the world around them.

"Do you want to love, Balthazar?" She pulled in a ragged breath. "Do you want to love me?"

"I do," he said, without pausing to consider it. Without worrying over the angles, the ramifications. And it all made sense then. All his broken pieces, all those feelings. The cacophony of the things that howled in him, louder by the second. And the fact that she was there in the middle of it all. The reason for everything. "I do."

And when she smiled, it was like daybreak. But better, because it was all his.

"Then don't worry," she told him. "Concentrate on what you're good at."

He brought her hands to his mouth and placed a kiss there. "If you mean passion, I do not think that will be a problem."

Her smile widened. "I believe you. But I don't mean passion. That's almost assured, I would think. No, Balthazar. I mean revenge."

"I will renounce it," he told her at once.

"But I don't want you to."

Kendra moved even closer, tipping her face back, so it was as if the whole world was her gaze. The press of her round belly into his body. Her hands he held in his.

Here on this altar where he had made her his wife.

"I want you to take your revenge, Balthazar," Kendra told him, solemn and sure. "The most perfect way possible. I want you to let me love you. I want you to love me in return. I want us to raise this child with joy."

"Joy," he repeated, like vows etched in stone.

"Not the way we were raised, always made to feel that we were never enough." She shook her head and her tears spilled over, but she was smiling. God help him, but he could watch that smile forever. He intended to do just that. "I want us to live life, big and bright and happy."

"Then that is what we will do," Balthazar promised her. "No matter what."

"That will be the ultimate revenge," Kendra said as she melted against him. "A life well lived, together."

And as he swept her up into his arms, the stars shone down, like a blessing. A promise.

Their true vows had finally been spoken.

And their real life began.

CHAPTER THIRTEEN

REVENGE CERTAINLY WAS SWEET, Kendra thought ten years later.

She sat in her favorite spot on the cozy sofa in Great-Aunt Rosemary's cottage in France. Outside it was a golden, glorious summer, which reminded her of her first months here. She smiled, remembering it. Pregnant without knowing it and so focused on choosing a new path in life. Treating strangers she waited on with kindness when she hardly knew how to offer the same to herself.

All without the slightest bit of knowledge of how profoundly her life was about to change, like it or not.

"I wish I'd known you better," she murmured to the room at large.

But she would have to settle for knowing

herself. And she thought her prickly great-aunt would have approved.

Outside, she could hear the approach of excited voices, and smiled even wider. She could pick them all out from each other, each voice like a new song in her heart. Serious, delightfully odd Irene, who had made Kendra a mother and made her laugh, daily. She was almost a decade old now, when Kendra could still remember the shock and miracle of her arrival. She had been born straight into her father's hands, and as if it were yesterday, Kendra recalled gazing at Balthazar over Irene's tiny, fragile head, the wonder almost too bright to bear.

It was still that bright.

"If we're going to have a family," Balthazar had said when Irene was still new, "then we might as well do it right."

"Is that a proclamation?" Kendra had asked, rolling her eyes at him, so dramatically she thought half of Athens must have seen.

But Balthazar only smiled.

Baz had been born in the following year, and Kendra grinned as she heard her oldest son shouting outside. Never one to pay attention to his older sister's proclamations, far too much like his father, and currently making noise simply because he could.

Because unlike his father, Baz would not be beaten. He would not be cut into pieces and shoved into a cold, iron box.

Kendra stood from the sofa and went to the door, throwing it open so she could see her family come toward her across the fields. The two oldest ones bickering, as they did. And behind them, the most beautiful man she'd ever seen or ever would, holding the youngest two. One in each arm. Five-year-old Kassandra, all stubborn cheeks and a pouty lip. And the sunny, giggly baby, Thaddeus, who was eighteen months old and had the rest of them—and the world—wrapped around his chubby little fingers.

They could have been a painting, Kendra thought. Walking across golden fields studded with lavender and sunflowers, and the Alps in the distance.

But this was the life that she and Balthazar had made, and it was far better than any painting. It was complicated. Sometimes painful. And most of all, theirs.

They had taught each other how to love, and while there was no part of that Kendra did not find rewarding, that didn't mean it hadn't hurt along the way.

"I love you," he had said the morning after their fateful wedding day, scowling at her as if the words caused him pain.

"I love you too," she had replied, frowning right back at him. "And note that I didn't say it like there was a gun in my back."

Slowly but surely, they learned.

They had stayed on the island for the rest of Kendra's pregnancy, because neither one of them wished to share their fledgling happiness with the world.

The world could wait. And it did.

"I love you," he had said, over and over, every single day, so that by the time Irene was born, there was no more scowling.

And it only got better from there.

Though soon, too soon, it was time to let the world in again.

It had not always been easy.

Kendra had seen her father and brother only once. She and Balthazar had gone back to Connecticut, where it had all begun. There had been one unpleasant conversation, after which Kendra washed her hands of them both.

Balthazar had pressed charges against Tommy. Her father had not been ruined financially, but the ensuing scandal had made him persona non grata in all the places that meant anything to him.

They both found there was a solace in that. Kendra accompanied Balthazar to the long-term care facility where his mother lived out her days, and sat with him as he told her that it was done. At long last, it was done.

And she felt certain that if the other woman could have forgiven her son, she would have.

But the true surprise was when Emily Cabot Connelly had put down her Valium, contacted her attorneys, and divorced her husband. As part of her settlement she claimed, among a great many other things, that gracious old house on its own point on Long Island Sound that she had brought to her marriage in the first place.

The first thing she did was invite her daughter and grandchildren to visit her there.

And it made Kendra glad that she and her mother had found a way to build bridges in these last ten years. They might not always understand each other, but they tried. No matter what, they tried.

In the end, Kendra thought as she stood in the doorway of her cottage and watched the love of her life and the four children they both adored beyond the telling of it draw close, that was happiness.

True happiness wasn't one thing. It wasn't static. It was layered and deep, forever changing in the light. It was all the colors, feelings and frustrations of each moment and the broader life around it, wound together into the same tight knot.

The secret to life wasn't holding that knot in one place. It was learning how to do the knotting in the first place and then keep doing it, day after day. Year after year. To get up when knocked down, brush herself off, and do it all over again.

Happiness was in the details. Joy was all around.

Balthazar smiled at her as he approached, because gone was that grim, cold, intimidating man she'd met long ago. This Balthazar smiled. He even laughed. He was still fierce in business, demanding in bed, but best of all, he was happy.

They were happy.

They had built on to the cottage over time, adding space for their family, but still maintaining Great-Aunt Rosemary's cozy aesthetic. Tonight, they ate together out beneath a trellis wrapped in wisteria, breathing in the glory of the Provence summer. Just as Kendra's favorite great-aunt must have done herself.

And after the children had gone to sleep, Kendra and Balthazar sat out there together. Beneath the quiet stars, Kendra took her favorite seat. His lap.

"You seem particularly pleased with yourself, *agápi mou*," Balthazar murmured, though his attention was on the line of her neck as he tasted his way down the length of it. "It makes me wonder what you can possibly be thinking about."

Kendra was thinking about that gazebo, long ago. How overwhelmed she'd been. How thunderstruck.

She was thinking of the night she'd surrendered her innocence on that desk in New York that they had returned to again and again over time. Christening it repeatedly, because they could. Because the heat between them only grew.

God, how it grew.

She was thinking of the island, where they spent as much time as they could, grounding themselves in the quiet. In the peace.

And using the altar where they'd made their vows, first to a priest and then to each other, as a touchstone. A talisman. A way to remind themselves who they were. Who they wanted to be, come what may.

"Tell me," Balthazar urged her, his voice dark and hot, and she could feel his smile against her skin.

"What am I always thinking about?" When he lifted his head, she smiled at him, more in love now that she'd ever known a person could be. And she could see the same reflected back at her, always. "Revenge, Balthazar. Sweet, sweet revenge."

"I love you," he told her.

"I love you, too," she whispered.

And then he showed her exactly how much he loved her, the way he always did, muffling her cries against his chest.

Just as Kendra showed him the same in return. The way she always would, until he groaned into the crook of her neck.

Because, as always, love was the best revenge of all.

* * * * *

LET'S TALK

Romance

For exclusive extracts, competitions
and special offers, find us online:

- **f** facebook.com/millsandboon
- 📷 @millsandboonuk
- 🐦 @millsandboon

Or get in touch on 0844 844 1351*

For all the latest titles coming soon,
visit millsandboon.co.uk/nextmonth

Want even more
ROMANCE?

Join our bookclub today!

'Mills & Boon books, the perfect way to escape for an hour or so.'

Miss W. Dyer

'Excellent service, promptly delivered and very good subscription choices.'

Miss A. Pearson

'You get fantastic special offers and the chance to get books before they hit the shops'

Mrs V. Hall

Visit millsandbook.co.uk/Bookclub and save on brand new books.

MILLS & BOON